George Saintsbury

Seventeenth Century Lyrics

George Saintsbury

Seventeenth Century Lyrics

ISBN/EAN: 9783744766418

Printed in Europe, USA, Canada, Australia, Japan

Cover: Foto ©Andreas Hilbeck / pixelio.de

More available books at **www.hansebooks.com**

SEVENTEENTH CENTURY LYRICS

EDITED BY

GEORGE SAINTSBURY, M.A., LL.D.

PROFESSOR OF RHETORIC AND ENGLISH LITERATURE
IN THE UNIVERSITY OF EDINBURGH

LONDON: RIVINGTONS

CONTENTS

Contents

Contents vii

Contents

INTRODUCTION

SOME experience in compiling selections has taught me that it is scarcely possible, so far as the reader is concerned, to take too little trouble in explaining the method on which they are compiled. I shall only say as briefly as possible that I have construed the term 'Seventeenth Century' liberally, but not, I hope, too liberally, by extending the *terminus a quo* a little into the sixteenth. The death of Dryden, the last singer for many years who really sang in anything but comic vein, coincides so exactly with the century's close that no trespass there was necessary, or possible. For the rest, I have seldom considered the familiarity, and never the strangeness, of the pieces I have chosen; that is to say, I have seldom been deterred from giving a place to anything that I thought superlatively good because it was already well known, and I have never allowed mere novelty of discovery to make up for the want of intrinsic goodness.   Much, if not most, of what is found here will be familiar ; but the selection is, I think, more varied and richer than any previous one on a similar scale and plan.   The word 'lyric' I have construed largely, not refusing it even to pieces in decasyllabic verse, which were notoriously intended, or which are obviously suitable, to be sung rather than said.   And if I have had any other guiding motive it has been to please myself; for in this case, at any rate—though to please oneself may not be a certain way of pleasing others—there is no second way which is more certain.   To attempt to suit all tastes is pretty certainly to succeed in misfitting most. By pleasing yourself you can at least be sure that there is one person satisfied—an argument which I do not lay down as universally applicable in questions of conduct, but only as probably reasonable in the making of literary selections such as this.   It can never be more convenient than in attempting to assemble, in a small space, if not the essence, at least some sufficient and characteristic samples, of so great a matter as the lyrical production of the English poets in the time which passed from the death of Spenser to that of Dryden.   For this time was, with the exception, and perhaps hardly with the exception, of another hundred years which are just closing, the most fertile period of anything like the same length in the literary history of England, and not inferior in quantity and quality of lyrical produce to any century in any other history. The exquisite contents of the Greek lyric anthology, even construing the word 'lyric' in the most generous way, are scattered over some thousand years : to make a really great collection of lyrics in Latin we must stride even more seven-leaguedly, and include mediæval hymns. The Scotch and Spanish lyres mostly give us folk-songs, delightful but hard to fix to any date. To get together any such collection as is here given in French, we must draw on every age from the twelfth century to the nineteenth. But in this seventeenth century of ours England was a mere nest of singing birds, a night-ingale's haunt in a centennial May.

It is rather a temptation to the abstract critic to inquire why it was that lyric properly so called was later than the other kinds in our Renaissance. That it was so is certain, and the fact, or a very little more than the fact, must suffice us here. It is not wholly improbable that the strong revulsion of the first genera-tion of Elizabethan poets of the best class from the old doggerel measures may have had something to do with it, but it is certain that the song proper, despite the passion of the age for music, was a little behind the drama, and considerably behind (I am taking the dates of perfection) the sonnet and the epic. Perhaps the retardation, slight as it was, helped the lyric impulse while it was finding way to gather the astounding volume and force which characterise it. The charming volumes in which Mr. A. H. Bullen has collected the lyrics of the Elizabethan song-books, romances, dramas, and what not, revealed for the first time to many what only a few knew before. But even a smattering of English letters must have informed any one who cared to let his brain work on the substance of his reading that the lyric gift grew in England from 1580, at least till 1660, with no small after-growths in Dryden, Sedley, and others, after a fashion hardly elsewhere to be paralleled. In the writers of this time we find one phenomenon recurring in the most unmistakable manner—the presence in men apparently of quite the second, third, or even a lower rank of literature, of an evidently natural gift which the very greatest men of another generation cannot reach though they seek it never so carefully. No competent judge, taking all things into consideration, would dream of setting such men as Campion, Carew, Herrick, Lovelace, and others on a par, as men of general literary faculty, with Swift, Pope, Thomson, even Gray. Yet the first batch, and even contemporaries of theirs much inferior to them, achieved lyrical effects which the latter cannot touch, cannot even approach unto, which never appear again until they are heard stammeringly in Cowper and fitfully in Coleridge. Take (and the comparison is crucial, for the Titanic craftsmanship of each was accompanied by greater learning in the one, and by a defter faculty of adjustment to the particular conditions in the other) Jonson and Dryden. Dryden's lyrics proper are, to my fancy, much undervalued, one main reason being that they lie chiefly in his plays, which nobody reads; and they are frequently charming. But where will you find in Dryden the exquisite touch of ' Drink to Me only with thine Eyes,' of ' Queen and Huntress,' of ' Underneath this sable Hearse '? You will no more find it than you will find in Jonson the flawless sweep of decasyllabic couplet, which in themes congenial enough of themselves to Ben drives home the argument in *Religio Laici,* makes history (and partisan-history) poetry in *Absalom and Achitophel,* and causes an ever-burning bush of ' singing flame ' to burgeon round Shadwell and Settle, Ferguson and Shaftesbury.

It is with the earlier and more fortunate period that we have mainly to busy ourselves. Besides the apparently (and only apparently) unphilosophical remarks that this lyrical spirit was here, that it broke out in the most unlikely places, and that in other and likely places we may seek for it in vain, there is really not much to say on the matter, in the way of assigning cause and effect, of examining whys and wherefores. Who has a more apparently lyrical imagination than John Ford? He has not left a single good lyric, and is probably responsible for some very bad ones. Who has a more elaborate and evidently conscientious theory of verse, which would, if carried out, make real English lyric impossible, than Thomas Campion? He has left us good store of work second only to the greatest efforts of the greatest masters. Who shall break into that incomparable and superhuman music, both sacred and profane, of 'I dare not ask a Kiss,' of 'The Litany,' of the 'Lines to Perilla'?— a decidedly reprobate parson, a rather vulgar-souled man in some ways, a foul-mouthed and foul-minded lampooner, a Philistine who would sooner have the *fumum et opes strepitumque* of Fleet Street than the loveliest country in England. Who shall soar into the Uranian passion of the 'St. Theresa' lines, and flutter in the playful grace of 'Whoe'er she be'?—a timid, self-centred Cambridge don, with hardly a thought outside his prayer-book and his college round of duties. Who shall accomplish the gorgeous eloquence of

> When thou, poor excommunicate,

the dewy freshness of

> Read in these roses the sad story?

—a fribble, a courtier, a debauchee, and if we may believe it, a man who wrote with difficulty and without inspiration.

There is no explanation of these things, or rather, the explanations fail to be explanatory to such an extent that, except as sets-off to critical conversation, we need not trouble ourselves about them. A few other matters properly within the purview of the critic and editor may demand a word or two. Although I cannot go the whole way with some critics who have thought that anapæstic and dactylic rhythm was unknown during this period (an opinion which, I am sure, they would have been as much delighted as I was to see changed by an anonymous writer into the dictum that 'rhymed anapæsts are not suited to the genius of our language'), it is certain that the great majority of the lyrists of this essentially lyrical age content themselves with the iamb and the trochee. And the secret, at least the metrical secret, of their success is the extraordinary effect which they get out of the soaring power of the one, and the liquid lapse of the other measure. Their iambs, nearly the last beat of which is heard in Sedley's famous lines—

> Love still has something of the sea
> From which his mother rose,

have the tower of the Theban eagle; their trochees, as in many an example of Ben and of the tribe of Ben, or in the 'King Pandion he is dead' of the *Passionate Pilgrim*, drip like honey from the rock. Even the magnificent imagination of Donne, the passion of Lovelace and Crashaw, the miraculous art of Carew, the dawn-lights of Herrick, depend to a great extent upon the command of these two staple measures,—a command which has been rather imitated than recovered since, and which is so marked and so unmistakable that it has acquired the name of 'the seventeenth century touch,' and is so spoken of whenever it is met in other men and other times.

Another point which may be worth making about this delightful vision of English literature is, that its effects, as far as thought and phrase, separated from metre, are concerned, are achieved partly by extreme simplicity, partly by excessive remoteness. Both are well-known means of arriving at that 'making of the common as though it were not common,' which is perhaps the best, and is certainly the most compendious definition of poetry. The simplicity-way is the most difficult, but the most effective; and it has never been applied with more success than by Shakespeare and the best of his followers in one way, by Jonson and the best of his followers in another. This is indeed the great glory of the period. Its greatest notoriety as distinguished from its greatest glory is derived from its exercises in the other extreme,—from those so-called 'metaphysical' eccentricities in language or in conceit which have been so often, if not always so justly, blamed, which have met with perhaps even more ridicule than blame, which certainly at their worst are ridiculous enough, and which yet at their best add a strange delight to the enjoyment of poetry. Of these things Donne is the unquestioned king; all others are but at best his well-willing subjects, at worst his clumsy courtiers and the imitators of his defects. It may be further observed that these conceits are nowhere so tolerable as in lyric. They are impertinent in narrative; they, to say the least, do not add to the verisimilitude of dramatic conversation; but within the short compass of a lyric they give, if happily handled, interest and flavour to the verse, and are capable of being accompanied and commented by the music in an unusual degree.[1]

As to the themes of the verse here collected, the chief of them is the theme of nine-tenths, of ninety-nine hundredths, of the lyrical poetry of the world. There are others, no doubt, and of some of them we shall find famous and admirable examples. But if it be not true that the lyre ἔρωτα μοῦνον ἠχεῖ, it sounds that passion so much more willingly, so much more happily than any other, that there can be no comparison of the results in volume or in merit. There are now—there always have been—plenty of denouncers of vain and amatorious poems; but few of them have the excuse of the author of the phrase that he could write as well as the amorists on

---

[1] It is sometimes thought bad manners to refer to one's own work; I hold it worse to repeat what has been elsewhere said. And I must therefore refer any one who wishes to see more on this 'metaphysical' subject to my *History of Elizabethan Literature*, chap. x.

themes other than erotic. In nine cases out of ten the impulse which makes a man spontaneously lyrical is the impulse of passion ; in ninety-nine cases out of a hundred the subject to which a man turns who not quite so spontaneously seeks a subject, is the same. But no age has ever been so happy in the love-lyric as this which we are studying, or so various in its fashion of treating it. Whether the poet lean to Venus Pandemos with Carew, or to Venus Urania with Crashaw ; whether he be whimsical with Suckling, heroically and simply passionate with Montrose and Lovelace, literary with Ben, half sensual, half spiritual, with Donne, almost wholly sensual, and yet not morbid, with Herrick, he seldom at his best misses those transporting touches which immortalise the commonplace needs of humanity, its usual pleasures, its weaknesses from the point of view of the philosopher; which half excuse its relapses into folly and sin from the point of view of the ascetic. There will be found here amply sufficient matter to vindicate this from being a book of mere love-songs ; but the mere love-songs will, I think, be found to be as much the best and the most immortal part of it as the emotions which they celebrate are, when all is said and done, the best things and the most immortal of life itself.

Of the other chief themes of lyric two—wine and war—are not extensively represented in our matter, though the latter has one inimitable and hardly surpassed example in Drayton's Ballad of Agincourt. The drinking-song is, for what reason I hardly know, seeing that we have until lately had the repute of being no ill hands at drinking, not very well represented at any time in English till the late and rather literary than spontaneous era of Moore and Peacock. One noble song, indeed the immortal

Back and side go bare, go bare,

which for the credit of the Church I hope Bishop Still did write, is much earlier than even a generous construction of our time can admit. Some bacchanals of Alexander Brome's in the full middle of it have merit. But for the most part Venus engaged the singers to the neglect of both her principal lovers. The political verse of the time finds a better place in another volume of this series, exclusively devoted to its class ; for political verse, though by no means a bastard kind, is one which keeps strictly to itself. Nor shall we find very much of the various kinds of comic or social verse which belong in their perfection to a further advanced and less simple state of manners and feelings.   Such verse, at any rate in the best time of our period, has for the most part a somewhat un-intentional comedy if it is playful merely, being 'metaphysical' in the dangerous way, and is brutally horse-playful if it is intended for downright satire.   The epigrams of Ben and his tribe are often lyrical in form, but Heaven forbid that any one should admit some of them to such a banquet of the Muses as I hope this will be.   On the other hand, the epitaph attained at this time, as is well known, to a perfection never afterwards rivalled in English, except once or twice by Landor, and never before even approached.   Religious verse is in the same condition.   Only Miss Christina Rossetti has since come near the union of real poetry and real religion which characterises Crashaw and Vaughan, Herrick and Donne.   And the time is not much less successful in the serious verse—moral or properly metaphysical—which comes closest to the religious division.   Though the sense of the picturesque was not supposed to be born, it is admirable in its descrip-tions of country life and joys.   But somehow or other it brings most of these things round to the one great theme—the central, the absorbing—of love,—love happy or unhappy, physical or metaphysical, but always Love.

In the following pages, though there is a certain regular chronological progress, I have not adopted, but have designedly disregarded exact chronological order, and have expressly eschewed putting all the selections from the same author together. If there is any drawback to this (and I really do not know what it is, as the index of authors with their dates must prevent any real confusion), it is, I think, more than compensated by the wild civility of the mixture of subjects and styles. I have avoided pieces of very great length, and this avoidance as well as its mainly political character has excluded one poem which I should like to have given—Marvell's *Horatian Ode*. Poems which could not be given without omissions have been eschewed; or perhaps I might say that I have found no difficulty in giving the whole of almost everything that I wished to give. No sonnets will be found here, for they seem to me, for all their beauty, among the least lyrical—that is to say, *singable* to music—of any poetic forms. Nor is there anything from Shakespeare or from Milton; for the stars look best when both sun and moon are away.

(1)

John Donne (?)

Absence, hear thou my protestation,
   Against thy strength,
   Distance, and length :
Do what thou canst for alteration,
  For hearts of truest mettle
  Absence doth join, and Time doth settle.

Who loves a mistress of such quality,
   He soon hath found
   Affection's ground
Beyond time, place, and all mortality.
  To hearts that cannot vary,
  Absence is present, Time doth tarry.

My senses want their outward motions,
   Which now within
   Reason doth win,
Redoubled in her secret notions :

B

Like rich men that take pleasure
In hiding, more than handling treasure.

By absence this good means I gain,
That I can catch her
Where none can watch her,
In some close corner of my brain.
There I embrace and kiss her;
And so I both enjoy and miss her.

(2)

MICHAEL DRAYTON.

FAIR stood the wind for France,
When we our sails advance,
Nor now to prove our chance,
    Longer will tarry;
But putting to the main,
At Caux, the mouth of Seine,
With all his martial train,
    Landed King Harry.

And taking many a fort,
Furnish'd in warlike sort,
Marcheth towards Agincourt
    In happy hour;
Skirmishing day by day
With those that stopp'd his way,
Where the French gen'ral lay
    With all his power.

Which in his height of pride,
King Henry to deride,
His ransom to provide
    To the king sending.
Which he neglects the while,
As from a nation vile,
Yet with an angry smile,
    Their fall portending.

And turning to his men,
Quoth our brave Henry then,
'Though they be one to ten,
    Be not amazed.
Yet have we well begun,
Battles so bravely won
Have ever to the Sun
    By fame been raised.

'As for myself,' quoth he,
'This my full rest shall be,
England ne'er mourn for me,
    Nor more esteem me.
Victor I will remain,
Or on this earth lie slain,
Never shall she sustain
    Loss to redeem me.

Michael Drayton

' Poitiers and Cressy tell,
When most their pride did swell,
Under our swords they fell,
        No less our skill is,
Than when our grandsire great,
Claiming the regal seat,
By many a warlike feat
        Lopp'd the French lilies.'

The Duke of York so dread,
The eager vaward led ;
With the main Henry sped,
        Amongst his henchmen.
Excester had the rear,
A braver man not there,
O Lord, how hot they were
        On the false Frenchmen !

They now to fight are gone,
Armour on armour shone,
Drum now to drum did groan,
        To hear, was wonder ;
That with the cries they make,
The very earth did shake,
Trumpet to trumpet spake,
        Thunder to thunder.

Well it thine age became,
O noble Erpingham,
Which didst the signal aim
    To our hid forces ;
When from a meadow by,
Like a storm suddenly,
The English archery
    Stuck the French horses.

With Spanish yew so strong,
Arrows a cloth-yard long,
That like to serpents stung,
    Piercing the weather ;
None from his fellow starts,
But playing manly parts,
And like true English hearts,
    Stuck close together.

When down their bows they threw,
And forth their bilbows drew,
And on the French they flew ;
    Not one was tardy ;
Arms were from shoulders sent,
Scalps to the teeth were rent,
Down the French peasants went,
    Our men were hardy.

This while our noble king,
His broad sword brandishing,
Down the French host did ding,
    As to o'erwhelm it ;
And many a deep wound lent,
His arms with blood besprent,
And many a cruel dent
    Bruised his helmet.

Glo'ster, that duke so good,
Next of the royal blood,
For famous England stood,
    With his brave brother,
Clarence, in steel so bright,
Though but a maiden knight,
Yet in that furious fight
    Scarce such another.

Warwick in blood did wade,
Oxford the foe invade,
And cruel slaughter made,
    Still as they ran up ;
Suffolk his axe did ply,
Beaumont and Willoughby
Bare them right doughtily,
    Ferrers and Fanhope.

Upon St. Crispin's day
Fought was this noble fray,
Which Fame did not delay,
    To England to carry;
O, when shall English men
With such acts fill a pen,
Or England breed again
    Such a King Harry!

(3)

ANONYMOUS.

THOU sent'st to me a heart was crowned ;
    I took it to be thine,
But when I saw it had a wound
    I knew that heart was mine.
A bounty of a strange conceit !
    To send mine own to me,
And send it in a worse estate
    Than when it came to thee.

(4)

JOHN DONNE.

WHOEVER comes to shroud me, do not harm
      Nor question much
That subtle wreath of hair about mine arm ;
The mystery, the sign, you must not touch,
      For 'tis my outward soul,
Viceroy to that, which unto Heav'n being gone,
      Will leave this to control,
And keep these limbs, these provinces from dissolu-
      tion.

For if the sinewy thread my brain lets fall
      Through every part,
Can tie those parts, and make me one of all ;
These hairs, which upward grow, and strength and art
      Have from a better brain,
Can better do 't : except she meant that I
      By this should know my pain,
As prisoners then are manacl'd, when they're con-
      demn'd to die.

Whate'er she meant by 't, bury it with me,
          For since I am
Love's martyr, it might breed idolatry,
If into other hands these relics came.
          As 'twas humility
T' afford to it all that a soul can do ;
          So 'tis some bravery,
That, since you would have none of me, I bury some
          of you.

(5)

THOMAS DEKKER.

Cold 's the wind, and wet 's the rain,
  Saint Hugh be our good speed !
Ill is the weather that bringeth no gain,
  Nor helps good hearts in need.

Troll the bowl, the jolly nut-brown bowl,
  And here, kind mate, to thee !
Let 's sing a dirge for Saint Hugh's soul,
  And down it merrily.

Down-a-down, hey, down-a-down,
  Hey derry derry down-a-down.
Ho ! well done, to me let come,
  Ring compass, gentle joy !
Troll the bowl, the nut-brown bowl,
      And here kind, etc.

Cold 's the wind, and wet 's the rain,
  Saint Hugh ! be our good speed ;
Ill is the weather that bringeth no gain,
  Nor helps good hearts in need.

(6)

FRANCIS DAVISON.

I

WIT's perfection, Beauty's wonder,
Nature's pride, the Graces' treasure,
Virtue's hope, his friends' sole pleasure,
This small marble stone lies under;
Which is often moist with tears,
For such loss in such young years.

II

Lovely boy! thou art not dead,
But from earth to heaven fled;
For base earth was far unfit
For thy beauty, grace, and wit.

III

Thou alive on earth, sweet boy,
Hadst an angel's wit and face;
And now dead, thou dost enjoy,
In high Heaven, an angel's place.

(7)

SIR WALTER RALEIGH (?)

As you came from the holy land
   Of Walsinghame,
Met you not with my true love
   By the way as you came?

How shall I know your true love,
   That have met many one,
As I went to the holy land,
   That have come, that have gone?

She is neither white nor brown,
   But as the heavens fair;
There is none hath a form so divine
   In the earth or the air.

Such a one did I meet, good sir,
   Such an angelic face,
Who like a queen, like a nymph, did appear,
   By her gate, by her grace.

She hath left me here all alone,
    All alone, as unknown,
Who sometimes did me lead with herself,
    And me loved as her own.

What's the cause that she leaves you alone,
    And a new way did take,
Who loved you once as her own,
    And her joy did you make?

I have loved her all my youth,
    But now old, as you see :
Love likes not the falling fruit
    From the withered tree.

Know that Love is a careless child,
    And forgets promise past ;
He is blind, he is deaf when he list,
    And in faith never fast.

His desire is a dureless content,
    And a trustless joy ;
He is won with a world of despair
    And is lost with a toy.

Of womenkind such indeed is the love,
  Or the word love abused,
Under which many childish desires
  And conceits are excused.

But true love is a durable fire,
  In the mind ever burning,
Never sick, never old, never dead,
  From itself never turning.

(8)

RICHARD BARNFIELD.

As it fell upon a day,
In the merry month of May,
Sitting in a pleasant shade,
Which a group of myrtles made,
Beasts did leap and birds did sing,
Trees did grow and plants did spring,
Everything did banish moan,
Save the nightingale alone ;
She, poor bird, as all forlorn,
Lean'd her breast against a thorn,
And there sung the dolefull'st ditty,
That to hear it was great pity.
Fie, fie, fie ! now would she cry ;
Teru, teru, by-and-by.
That to hear her so complain
Scarce I could from tears refrain,
For her griefs so lively shown
Made me think upon mine own.

Ah, thought I, thou mourn'st in vain,
None takes pity on thy pain.
Senseless trees, they cannot hear thee;
Ruthless beasts, they will not cheer thee;
King Pandion he is dead,
All thy friends are lapp'd in lead;
All thy fellow birds do sing,
Careless of thy sorrowing;
Even so, poor bird, like thee,
None alive will pity me.

Ben Jonson

is in matters dif. fr. the usual Trochaic-iambus [19] of the
♂ — They have many Pyrrhics, & their long-syll. a
shortish. Here the longs are long broad or
✓ often.   May 7/'13.

(9)

BEN JONSON.

QUEEN, and Huntress, chaste and fair,
Now the sun is laid to sleep,
Seated in thy silver chair,
State in wonted manner keep :
    Hesperus entreats thy light,
    Goddess excellently bright.

Earth, let not thy envious shade
Dare itself to interpose ;
Cynthia's shining orb was made
Heav'n to clear, when day did close :
    Bless us then with wishèd sight
    Goddess excellently bright.

Lay thy bow of pearl apart,
And thy shining crystal quiver ;
Give unto the flying hart
Space to breathe, how short soever :
    Thou that mak'st a day of night
    Goddess excellently bright.

(10)

JOHN DONNE.

DEAR love, for nothing less than thee
Would I have broke this happy dream,
          It was a theme
For reason, much too strong for fantasy.
Therefore thou wak'dst me wisely; yet
My dream thou brok'st not, but continu'dst it:
Thou art so true, that thoughts of thee suffice
To make dreams truth, and fables histories;
Enter these arms, for since thou thought'st it best
Not to dream all my dream, let 's act the rest.

As lightning or a taper's light
Thine eyes, and not thy noise, wak'd me.
          Yet I thought thee
(For thou lov'st truth) an angel at first sight,
But when I saw thou saw'st my heart,
And knew'st my thoughts beyond an angel's art,

When thou knew'st what I dreamt, then thou knewest
    when
Excess of joy would wake me, and cam'st then;
I must confess, it could not choose but be
Profane to think thee anything but thee.

Coming and staying show'd thee thee,
But rising makes me doubt, that now
        Thou art not thou.
That love is weak, where fear 's as strong as he;
'Tis not all spirit, pure and brave,
If mixture it of fear, shame, honour, have,
Perchance as torches, which must ready be,
Men light and put out, so thou deal'st with me,
Thou cam'st to kindle, goest to come: then I
Will dream that hope again, but else would die.

(11)

THOMAS CAMPION.

FOLLOW your saint, follow with accents sweet !
Haste you, sad notes, fall at her flying feet !
There, wrapped in cloud of sorrow, pity move,
And tell the ravisher of my soul I perish for her love :
But, if she scorns my never-ceasing pain,
Then burst with sighing in her sight, and ne'er return
      again.

All that I sang still to her praise did tend,
Still she was first, still she my songs did end ;
Yet she my love and music both doth fly,
The music that her echo is and beauty's sympathy :
Then let my notes pursue her scornful flight ;
It shall suffice that they were breathed and died for
      her delight.

(12)

ANONYMOUS.

WE be soldiers three,
Pardona moy je vous an pree,
Lately come forth of the Low Country
With never a penny of money.
      Fa la la la lantido dilly.

Here, good fellow, I drink to thee,
Pardona moy je vous an pree,
To all good fellows wherever they be,
With never a penny of money.

And he that will not pledge me this,
Pardona moy je vous an pree,
Pays for the shot whatever it is,
With never a penny of money.

Charge it again, boy, charge it again,
Pardona moy je vous an pree,
As long as there is any ink in thy pen
With never a penny of money.

(13)

BEN JONSON.

WEEP with me, all you that read
    This little story :
And know, for whom a tear you shed
    Death's self is sorry.
'Twas a child that so did thrive
    In grace and feature,
As Heaven and Nature seemed to strive
    Which owned the creature.
Years he numbered scarce thirteen
    When Fates turned cruel,
Yet three filled zodiacs he had been
    The stage's jewel ;
And did act, what now we moan,
    Old men so duly,
As, sooth, the Parcae thought him one,
    He played so truly.
So, by error to his fate
    They all consented ;
But viewing him since, alas, too late
    They have repented ;
And have sought to give new birth,
    In baths to steep him ;
But being so much too good for earth
    Heaven vows to keep him.

(14)

SIR WALTER RALEIGH.

GIVE me my scallop-shell of quiet,
  My staff of faith to walk upon,
My scrip of joy, immortal diet,
  My bottle of salvation,
My gown of glory, hope's true gaze;
And thus I'll take my pilgrimage.

Blood must be my body's balmer;
  No other balm will there be given;
Whilst my soul, like quiet palmer,
  Travelleth towards the land of heaven;
Over the silver mountains,
Where spring the nectar fountains:
    There will I kiss
    The bowl of bliss;
And drink mine everlasting fill
Upon every milken hill.

My soul will be a-dry before;
But after, it will thirst no more.
Then by that happy blissful day,
    More peaceful pilgrims I shall see,
That have cast off their rags of clay,
    And walked apparelled fresh like me.
        I'll take them first
        To quench their thirst
And taste of nectar suckets,
        At those clear wells
        Where sweetness dwells
Drawn up by saints in crystal buckets.

And when our bottles and all we
Are filled with immortality,
Then the blessed paths we'll travel,
Strowed with rubies thick as gravel;
Ceilings of diamonds, sapphire floors,
High walls of coral, and pearly bowers.
From thence to heaven's bribeless hall,
Where no corrupted voices brawl;
No conscience molten into gold,
No forged accuser bought or sold.
No cause deferred, no vain-spent journey;
For there Christ is the King's Attorney,
Who pleads for all without degrees,
And He hath Angels, but no fees.

And when the grand twelve million jury
Of our sins, with direful fury,
    Against our souls black verdicts give,
    Christ pleads His death, and then we live.

Be Thou my speaker, taintless pleader,
Unblotted lawyer, true proceeder !
Thou givest salvation even for alms ;
Not with a bribed lawyer's palms.
    And this is mine eternal plea
    To Him that made heaven, and earth, and sea,
    That, since my flesh must die so soon,
    And want a head to dine next noon,
Just at the stroke, when my veins start and spread,
Set on my soul an everlasting head !
    Then am I ready, like a palmer fit,
    To tread those blest paths which before I writ.

Of death and judgment, heaven and hell,
Who oft doth think, must needs die well.

(15)

ANONYMOUS.

WE be three poor mariners,
  Newly come from the seas ;
We spend our lives in jeopardy
  While others live at ease.
Shall we go dance the round, the round,
  Shall we go dance the round?
And he that is a bully boy
  Come pledge me on this ground !

We care not for those martial men
  That do our states disdain ;
But we care for the merchant men
  Who do our states maintain :
To them we dance this round, around,
  Shall we go dance the round?
And he that is a bully boy
  Come pledge me on this ground !

(16)

JOHN DONNE.

Go, and catch a falling star,
　Get with child a mandrake root,
Tell me where all times past are,
　Or who cleft the Devil's foot.
Teach me to hear mermaids singing,
Or to keep off envy's stinging,
　　　And find,
　　　What wind
Serves to advance an honest mind.

If thou be'st born to strange sights,
　Things invisible go see,
Ride ten thousand days and nights,
　Till age snow white hairs on thee.
Thou, when thou return'st, will tell me
All strange wonders, that befell thee,
　　　And swear,
　　　Nowhere

Lives a woman true and fair.

If thou find'st one, let me know,
   Such a pilgrimage were sweet ;
Yet do not, I would not go,
   Though at next door we might meet.
Though she were true when you met her,
And last, till you write your letter,
       Yet she
       Will be
False, ere I come, to two or three.

(17)

BEN JONSON.

DRINK to me only with thine eyes,
  And I will pledge with mine;
Or leave a kiss within the cup,
  And I'll not look for wine.
The thirst that from the soul doth rise,
  Doth ask a drink divine:
But might I of Jove's nectar sup,
  I would not change for thine.
I sent thee late a rosy wreath,
  Not so much honouring thee,
As giving it a hope, that there
  It could not withered be.
But thou thereon didst only breathe,
  And sent'st it back to me:
Since when it grows, and smells, I swear,
  Not of itself, but thee.

(18)

SIR WALTER RALEIGH

EVEN such is time, that takes in trust
   Our youth, our joys, our all we have,
And pays us but with earth and dust ;
   Who, in the dark and silent grave,
When we have wandered all our ways,
Shuts up the story of our days ;
But from this earth, this grave, this dust
My God shall raise me up I trust !

(19)

NICHOLAS BRETON.

In the merry month of May,
In a morn by break of day,
Forth I walk'd by the wood-side,
When as May was in his pride:
There I spièd all alone,
Phyllida and Corydon.
Much ado there was, God wot!
He would love and she would not.
She said never man was true;
He said, none was false to you.
He said, he had loved her long;
She said, Love should have no wrong.
Corydon would kiss her then;
She said, maids must kiss no men,
Till they did for good and all;
Then she made the shepherd call
All the heavens to witness truth
Never loved a truer youth.

Thus with many a pretty oath,
Yea and nay, and faith and troth,
Such as silly shepherds use
When they will not Love abuse,
Love which had been long deluded,
Was with kisses sweet concluded ;
And Phyllida, with garlands gay,
Was made the lady of the May.

(20)

WALTER DAVISON.

AT her fair hands how have I grace entreated,
    With prayers oft repeated !
    Yet still my love is thwarted :
Heart, let her go, for she 'll not be converted.
    Say, shall she go?
    Oh ! no, no, no, no, no ;
She is most fair, though she be marble-hearted.

How often have my sighs declared mine anguish,
    Wherein I daily languish !
    Yet doth she still procure it :
Heart, let her go, for I cannot endure it.
    Say, shall she go ?
    Oh ! no, no, no, no, no ;
She gave the wound, and she alone must cure it.

The trickling tears that down my cheeks have flowed,
    My love have often showed ;
    Yet still unkind I prove her :

Heart, let her go, for nought I do can move her.
   Say, shall she go?
   Oh! no, no, no, no, no;
Though me she hates, I cannot choose but love her.

But shall I still a true affection owe her,
    Which prayers, sighs, tears, do show her,
    And shall she still disdain me?
Heart, let her go, if they no grace can gain me.
   Say, shall she go?
   Oh! no, no, no, no, no;
She made me hers, and hers she will retain me.

But if the love that hath, and still doth burn me,
    No love at length return me,
    Out of my thoughts I'll set her.
Heart, let her go; oh heart! I pray thee, let her.
   Say, shall she go?
   Oh! no, no, no, no, no;
Fixed in the heart, how can the heart forget her?

But if I weep and sigh, and often wail me,
    Till tears, sighs, prayers, fail me,
    Shall yet my love persever?
Heart, let her go, if she will right thee never.
   Say, shall she go?
   Oh! no, no, no, no, no;
Tears, sighs, prayers, fail; but true love lasteth ever.

(21)

THOMAS DEKKER.

ART thou poor, yet hast thou golden slumbers?
   Oh, sweet content!
 Art thou rich, yet is thy mind perplexed?
   Oh, punishment!
Dost thou laugh to see how fools are vexed
To add to golden numbers, golden numbers?
   Oh, sweet content!   Oh, sweet content!

Work apace, apace, apace, apace;
Honest labour bears a lovely face;
Then hey noney, noney, hey noney, noney.

Canst drink the waters of the crispèd spring?
   Oh, sweet content!
 Swimmest thou in wealth, yet sinkest in thine
   own tears?
   Oh, punishment!
Then he that patiently want's burden bears,
No burden bears, but is a king, a king!
   Oh, sweet content!   Oh, sweet content!

Work apace, apace, etc.

(22)

THOMAS CAMPION.

AWAKE, awake! thou heavy sprite
  That sleep'st the deadly sleep of sin!
Rise now and walk the ways of light,
  'Tis not too late yet to begin.
Seek heaven early, seek it late;
True Faith finds still an open gate.

Get up, get up, thou leaden man!
  Thy track to endless joy or pain,
Yields but the model of a span:
  Yet burns out thy life's lamp in vain!
One minute bounds thy bane or bliss;
Then watch and labour while time is.

(23)

JOHN DONNE.

IF yet I have not all thy love,
Dear, I shall never have it all,
I cannot breathe one other sigh, to move;
Nor can intreat one other tear to fall;
And all my treasure, which should purchase thee,
Sighs, tears, and oaths, and letters I have spent;
Yet no more can be due to me,
Than at the bargain made was meant:
If then thy gift of love was partial,
That some for me, some should to others fall,
    Dear, I shall never have it all.

Or, if then thou giv'st me all,
All was but all, which thou hadst then:
But if in thy heart since there be, or shall
New love created be by other men,
Which have their stocks entire, and can in tears,
In sighs, in oaths, in letters outbid me,
This new love may beget new fears,

For this love was not vow'd by thee.
And yet it was thy gift being general;
The ground, thy heart, is mine, whatever shall
    Grow there, dear, I should have it all.

Yet I would not have all yet,
He that hath all can have no more,
And since my love doth every day admit
New growth, thou should'st have new rewards in store;
Thou canst not every day give me thy heart,
If thou canst give it, then thou never gav'st it :
Love's riddles are, that though thy heart depart,
It stays at home, and thou with losing sav'st it :
But we will love a way more liberal,
Than changing hearts, to join us, so we shall
    Be one, and one another's all.

(24)

BEN JONSON.

SOME act of Love's bound to rehearse,
I thought to bind him in my verse:
Which when he felt, Away, quoth he,
Can poets hope to fetter me?
It is enough, they once did get
Mars and my mother, in their net:
I wear not these my wings in vain.
With which he fled me; and again,
Into my rhymes could ne'er be got
By any art: then wonder not,
That since, my numbers are so cold,
When Love is fled, and I am old.

(25)

ROBERT JONES.

THE sea hath many a thousand sands,
The sun hath motes as many;
The sky is full of stars, and love
As full of woes as any:
Believe me, that do know the elf,
And make no trial by thyself.

It is in truth a pretty toy
For babes to play withal;
But O, the honeys of our youth
Are oft our age's gall!
Self-proof in time will make thee know
He was a prophet told thee so:

A prophet that, Cassandra-like,
Tells truth without belief;
For headstrong youth will run his race,
Although his goal be grief:
Love's martyr, when his heat is past,
Proves Care's confessor at the last.

(26)

THOMAS DEKKER.

CAST away care; he that loves sorrow
Lengthens not a day, nor can buy to-morrow;
Money is trash; and he that will spend it,
Let him drink merrily, Fortune will send it.
　　Merrily, merrily, merrily, Oh, ho!
　　Play it off stiffly, we may not part so.

Wine is a charm, it heats the blood too,
Cowards it will arm, if the wine be good too;
Quickens the wit, and makes the back able,
Scorns to submit to the watch or constable.
　　　　　　Merrily, etc.

Pots fly about, give us more liquor,
Brothers of a rout, our brains will flow quicker;
Empty the cask; score up, we care not;
Fill all the pots again; drink on, and spare not.
　　　　　　Merrily, etc.

(27)

BEN JONSON.

COME, my Celia, let us prove,
While we may, the sports of love;
Time will not be ours for ever:
He at length our good will sever.
Spend not then his gifts in vain,
Suns that set may rise again;
But if once we lose this light,
'Tis with us perpetual night.
Why should we defer our joys?
Fame and rumour are but toys.
Cannot we delude the eyes
Of a few poor household spies;
Or his easier ears beguile,
So removed by our wile?
'Tis no sin love's fruit to steal,
But the sweet theft to reveal:
To be taken, to be seen,
These have crimes accounted been.

(28)

BEN JONSON.

Kiss me, sweet : the wary lover
Can your favours keep, and cover,
When the common courting jay
All your bounties will betray.
Kiss again : no creature comes.
Kiss, and score up wealthy sums
On my lips thus hardly sundered,
While you breathe.   First give a hundred.
Then a thousand, then another
Hundred, then unto the other
Add a thousand, and so more :
Till you equal with the store,
All the grass that Rumney yields,
Or the sands in Chelsea fields,
Or the drops in silver Thames,
Or the stars that gild his streams,
In the silent summer nights,
When youths ply their stolen delights ;
That the curious may not know
How to tell 'em as they flow,
And the envious, when they find
What their number is, be pined.

(29)

THOMAS CAMPION.

I CARE not for these ladies
 That must be wooed and prayed,
Give me kind Amaryllis,
 The wanton country maid :
Nature art disdaineth,
Her beauty is her own :
  Her when we court and kiss,
  She cries, 'Forsooth, let go !'
  But when we come where comfort is,
  She never will say 'No.'

If I love Amaryllis,
 She gives me fruit and flowers ;
But if we love these ladies,
 We must give golden showers.
Give them gold that sell love,
Give me the nut-brown lass,

Who when we court and kiss,
She cries, 'Forsooth, let go!'
But when we come where comfort is,
She never will say 'No.'

These ladies must have pillows
   And beds by strangers wrought;
Give me a bower of willows,
   Of moss and leaves unbought;
And fresh Amaryllis,
With milk and honey fed,
      Who when we court and kiss,
      She cries, 'Forsooth, let go!'
      But when we come where comfort is,
      She never will say 'No.'

(30)

Anonymous.

My Love in her attire doth show her wit,
 It doth so well become her :
For every season she hath dressings fit,
  For Winter, Spring, and Summer.
  No beauty she doth miss,
  When all her robes are on :
  But Beauty's self she is,
  When all her robes are gone.

(31)

BEN JONSON.

NOT to know vice at all, and keep true state,
    Is virtue and not Fate :
Next to that virtue, is to know vice well,
    And her black spite expel.
Which to effect (since no breast is so sure,
    Or safe, but she 'll procure
Some way of entrance) we must plant a guard
    Of thoughts to watch and ward.

At the eye and ear, the ports unto the mind,
    That no strange or unkind
Object arrive there, but the heart, our spy,
    Give knowledge instantly,
To wakeful reason, our affections' king :
    Who, in th' examining,
Will quickly taste the treason, and commit
    Close, the close cause of it.
'Tis the securest policy we have,
    To make our sense our slave.

But this true course is not embraced by many :
      By many ! scarce by any.
For either our affections do rebel,
      Or else the sentinel,
That should ring 'larum to the heart, doth sleep ;
      Or some great thought doth keep
Back the intelligence, and falsely swears
      They are base and idle fears
Whereof the loyal conscience so complains.
      Thus, by these subtle trains,
Do several passions invade the mind,
      And strike our reason blind,
Of which usurping rank, some have thought love
      The first ; as prone to move
Most frequent tumults, horrors, and unrests
      In our enflamed breasts :
But this doth from the cloud of error grow,
      Which thus we over-blow.
The thing they here call Love, is blind Desire,
      Armed with bow, shafts, and fire ;
Inconstant, like the sea, of whence 'tis born,
      Rough, swelling, like a storm :
With whom, who sails, rides on the surge of fear,
      And boils, as if he were
In a continual tempest.   Now, true Love
      No such effects doth prove ;
That is an essence far more gentle, fine,
      Pure, perfect, nay divine ;

It is a golden chain let down from heaven,
    Whose links are bright and even,
That falls like sleep on lovers, and combines
    The soft, and sweetest minds
In equal knots : this bears no brands nor darts,
    To murther different hearts,
But in a calm and godlike unity
    Preserves community.
O, who is he that in this peace enjoys
    The Elixir of all joys?
A form more fresh than are the Eden bowers.
    And lasting as her flowers :
Richer than Time, and as Time's virtue rare :
    Sober, as saddest care ;
A fixed thought, an eye untaught to glance :
    Who, blest with such high chance,
Would, at suggestion of a steep desire,
    Cast himself from the spire
Of all his happiness?   But soft, I hear
    Some vicious fool draw near,
That cries we dream, and swears there's no such
    thing
    As this chaste love we sing.
Peace, Luxury, thou art like one of those
    Who, being at sea, suppose,
Because they move, the continent doth so.
    No, vice, we let thee know,
Though thy wild thoughts with sparrows' wings do fly;

Turtles can chastly die ;
And yet (in this t' express ourselves more clear)
    We do not number here
Such spirits as are only continent,
    Because lust's means are spent :
Or those who doubt the common mouth of fame,
    And for their place and name,
Cannot so safely sin : their chastity
    Is mere necessity.
Nor mean we those who vows and conscience
    Have filled with abstinence :
Though we acknowledge, who can so abstain,
    Makes a most blessed gain.
He that for love of goodness hateth ill,
    Is more crown-worthy still,
Than he which for sin's penalty forbears ;
    His heart sins, though he fears.
But we propose a person like our Dove,
    Graced with a Phoenix love ;
A beauty of that clear and sparkling light,
    Would make a day of night,
And turn the blackest sorrows to bright joys ;
    Whose odorous breath destroys
All taste of bitterness, and makes the air
    As sweet as she is fair.
A body so harmoniously composéd,
    As if Nature disclosed
All her best symmetry in that one feature !

O, so divine a creature,
Who could be false to? chiefly when he knows
How only she bestows
The wealthy treasure of her love on him;
Making his fortunes swim
In the full flood of her admired perfection?
What savage, brute affection,
Would not be fearful to offend a dame
Of this excelling frame?
Much more a noble and right generous mind,
To virtuous moods inclined,
That knows the weight of guilt, he will refrain
From thoughts of such a strain,
And to his sense object this sentence ever,
'Man may securely sin, but safely never.'

(32)

BEAUMONT AND FLETCHER.

LAY a garland on my hearse
    Of the dismal yew;
Maidens willow branches bear;
    Say, I died true.

My love was false, but I was firm
    From my hour of birth.
Upon my buried body lie
    Lightly, gentle earth!

(33)

BEN JONSON.

FAIR friend, 'tis true your beauties move
  My heart to a respect,
Too little to be paid with love,
  Too great for your neglect.

I neither love, nor yet am free,
  For though the flame I find
Be not intense in the degree,
  'Tis of the purest kind.

It little wants of love but pain ;
  Your beauty takes my sense,
And lest you should that price disdain,
  My thoughts too feel the influence.

'Tis not a passion's first access
  Ready to multiply ;
But like love's calmest state it is
  Possessed with victory.

It is like love to truth reduced,
  All the false values gone,
Which were created and induced
  By fond imagination.

'Tis either fancy or 'tis fate,
  To love you more than I :
I love you at your beauty's rate,
  Less were an injury.

Like unstamped gold, I weigh each grace,
  So that you may collect
Th' intrinsic value of your face,
  Safely from my respect.

And this respect would merit love,
  Were not so fair a sight
Payment enough ; for who dare move
  Reward for his delight ?

(34)

BEAUMONT AND FLETCHER.

CUPID, pardon what is past,
And forgive our sins at last!
Then we will be coy no more,
But thy deity adore;
Troths at fifteen we will plight,
And will tread a dance each night,
In the fields, or by the fire,
With the youths that have desire.
Given ear-rings we will wear,
Bracelets of our lovers' hair,
Which they on our arms shall twist,
With their names carved, on our wrist;
All the money that we owe
We in tokens will bestow;
And learn to write that, when 'tis sent,
Only our loves know what is meant.
　　　Oh, then pardon what is past,
　　　And forgive our sins at last.

(35)

SIR HENRY WOTTON.

YOU meaner beauties of the night,
  That poorly satisfy our eyes
More by your number than your light,
  You common people of the skies ;
  What are you when the moon shall rise ?

You curious chanters of the wood,
  That warble forth Dame Nature's lays,
Thinking your passions understood
  By your weak accents ; what 's your praise,
  When Philomel her voice shall raise ?

You violets that first appear,
  By your pure purple mantles known
Like the proud virgins of the year,
  As if the spring were all your own ;
  What are you when the rose is blown ?

So, when my mistress shall be seen
  In form and beauty of her mind,
By virtue first, then choice, a Queen,
  Tell me if she were not designed
  The eclipse and glory of her kind ?

(36)

JOHN FLETCHER.

FROM thy forehead thus I take
These herbs, and charge thee not awake
Till in yonder holy well
Thrice, with powerful magic spell,
Filled with many a baleful word,
Thou hast been dipped.   Thus, with my cord
Of blasted hemp, by moonlight twined,
I do thy sleepy body bind.
I turn thy head unto the east,
And thy feet unto the west,
Thy left arm to the south put forth,
And thy right unto the north.
I take thy body from the ground,
In this deep and deadly swound,
And into this holy spring
I let thee slide down by my string.
Take this maid, thou holy pit,
To thy bottom ; nearer yet ;

In thy water pure and sweet,
By thy leave I dip her feet ;
Thus I let her lower yet,
That her ankles may be wet ;
Yet down lower, let her knee
In thy waters washed be.
There stop.   Fly away,
Everything that loves the day !
Truth, that hath but one face,
Thus I charm thee from this place.
Snakes that cast your coats for new,
Chameleons that alter hue,
Hares that yearly sexes change,
Proteus altering oft and strange,
Hecatè, with shapes three,
Let this maiden changed be,
With this holy water wet,
To the shape of Amoret !
Cynthia work thou with my charm !
Thus I draw thee, free from harm,
Up out of this blessed lake.
Rise both like her and awake !

(37)

John Webster.

CALL for the robin redbreast and the wren,
Since o'er shady groves they hover,
And with leaves and flowers do cover
The friendless bodies of unburied men.
Call unto his funeral dole
The ant, the field-mouse, and the mole,
To rear him hillocks that shall keep him warm,
And (when gay tombs are robbed) sustain no harm;
But keep the wolf far thence, that 's foe to men,
For with his nails he 'll dig them up again.

(38)

BEAUMONT AND FLETCHER.

TELL me, dearest, what is love?
'Tis a lightning from above;
'Tis an arrow, 'tis a fire,
'Tis a boy they call Desire.
     'Tis a grave,
     Gapes to have
The poor fools who long to prove.

Tell me more, are women true?
Yes, some are, and some as you.
Some are willing, some are strange,
Since you men first taught to change.
     And till troth
     Be in both,
All shall love, to love anew.

Tell me more yet, can they grieve
Yes, and sicken sore, but live
And be wise, and delay,
When you men are wise as they.
     Then I see,
     Faith will be,
Never till they both believe.

THOMAS CAMPION.

KIND are her answers,
But her performance keeps no day;
Breaks time, as dancers,
From their own music when they stray.
All her free favours and smooth words
Wing my hopes in vain.
O, did ever voice so sweet but only feign?
Can true love yield such delay,
Converting joy to pain?

Lost is our freedom
When we submit to women so:
Why do we need 'em
When, in their best, they work our woe?
There is no wisdom
Can alter ends by Fate prefixt.
O, why is the good of man with evil mixt?
Never were days yet callèd two
But one night went betwixt.

(40)

ANONYMOUS.

OH ! what a pain is love,
How shall I bear it ?
She will inconstant prove,
I greatly fear it.
She so torments my mind,
That my strength faileth ;
And wavers with the wind,
As a ship that saileth.
Please her the best I may,
She looks another way,
Alack and well a day
       Phillada flouts me.

All the fair yesterday,
She did pass by me ;
She looked another way,
And would not spy me.
I wooed her for to dine,
But could not get her.
Will had her to the wine,
He might intreat her.

With Daniel she did dance,
On me she looked askance.
Oh thrice unhappy chance !
    Phillada flouts me.

Fair maid be not so coy,
Do not disdain me :
I am my mother's joy,
Sweet, entertain me.
She 'll give me when she dies,
All that is fitting,
Her poultry and her bees
And her geese sitting.
A pair of mattress beds,
And a bag full of shreds.
And yet for all this goods,
    Phillada flouts me.

She hath a clout of mine
Wrought with good Coventry,
Which she keeps for a sign
Of my fidelity.
But i' faith, if she flinch,
She shall not wear it.
To Tibb, my t'other wench,
I mean to bear it.
And yet it grieves my heart,
So soon from her to part.

Death strikes me with his dart,
    Phillada flouts me.

Thou shalt eat curds and cream,
All the year lasting ;
And drink the crystal stream,
Pleasant in tasting ;
Wigge and whey whilst thou burst
And ramble berry ;
Pie-lid and pasty-crust,
Pears, plums, and cherry.
Thy raiment shall be thin,
Made of a weaver's skin,
Yet all 's not worth a pin,
      Phillada flouts me.

Fair maidens, have a care,
And in time take me :
I can have those as fair,
If you forsake me.
For Doll the dairy-maid,
Laughed on me lately,
And wanton Winifred
Favours me greatly.
One throws milk on my clothes,
T'other plays with my nose ;
What wanton signs are those ?
      Phillada flouts me.

I cannot work and sleep
All at a season;
Love wounds my heart so deep,
Without all reason.
I 'gin to pine away,
With grief and sorrow,
Like to a fatted beast,
Penned in a meadow.
I shall be dead, I fear,
Within this thousand year;
And all for very fear,
      Phillada flouts me.

(41)

JOHN FLETCHER.

BEAUTY clear and fair,
    Where the air
Rather like a perfume dwells;
    Where the violet and the rose
    Their blue veins in blush disclose,
And come to honour nothing else.

Where to live near,
    And planted there,
Is to live, and still live new;
    Where to gain a favour is
    More than light, perpetual bliss,—
Make me live by serving you.

Dear, again back recall
    To this light,
A stranger to himself and all;
    Both the wonder and the story
    Shall be yours, and eke the glory:
I am your servant, and your thrall.

How they resemble each other!
In verse trochee & iamb—
In thought — light love of many wo...
In form sentimental philandering &
(42) rather broad

ROBERT HERRICK.

I HAVE lost, and lately, these
Many dainty mistresses :
Stately Julia, prime of all ;
Sappho next, a principal :
Smooth Anthea, for a skin
White, and heaven-like crystalline :
Sweet Electra, and the choice
Myrrha, for the lute, and voice.
Next, Corinna, for her wit,
And the graceful use of it :
With Perilla : all are gone.
Only Herrick 's left alone,
For to number sorrow by
Their departures hence, and die.

(43)

JOHN FLETCHER

CAST our caps and cares away:
This is beggars' holiday!
At the crowning of our king,
Thus we ever dance and sing.
In the world look out and see,
Where 's so happy a prince as he?
Where the nation lives so free,
And so merry do as we?
Be it peace, or be it war,
Here at liberty we are,
And enjoy our ease and rest:
To the field we are not pressed;
Nor are called into the town,
To be troubled with the gown.
Hang all offices, we cry,
And the magistrate too, by!
When the subsidy 's increased,
We are not a penny sessed;
Nor will any go to law
With the beggar for a straw.
All which happiness, he brags,
He doth owe unto his rags.

(44)

THOMAS RANDOLPH.

FAIR lady, when you see the grace
Of beauty in your looking-glass :
A stately forehead, smooth and high,
And full of princely majesty :
A sparkling eye, no gem so fair,
Whose lustre dims the Cyprian star :
A glorious cheek divinely sweet,
Wherein both roses kindly meet :
A cherry lip that would entice
Even gods to kiss at any price :
You think no beauty is so rare
That with your shadow might compare ;
That your reflection is alone
The thing that men most dote upon.
Madam, alas ! your glass doth lie,
And you are much deceived ; for I
A beauty know of richer grace
(Sweet, be not angry)—'tis your face.

Hence then, O, learn more mild to be,
And leave to lay your blame on me ;
If me your real substance move,
When you so much your shadow love,
Wise Nature would not let your eye
Look on her own bright majesty,
Which had you once but gazed upon,
You could, except yourself, love none :
What then you cannot love, let me—
That face I can—you cannot, see.
Now you have what to love, you 'll say,
What then is left for me, I pray ?
My face, sweetheart, if it please thee—
That which you can—I cannot, see.
So either love shall gain his due.
Yours, sweet, in me, and mine in you.

(45)

WILLIAM ROWLEY.

ART thou gone in haste?
  I 'll not forsake thee;
Runn'st thou ne'er so fast,
  I 'll o'ertake thee:
O'er the dales, o'er the downs,
  Through the green meadows,
From the fields through the towns,
  To the dim shadows.

All along the plain,
  To the low fountains,
Up and down again
  From the high mountains;
Echo then shall again
  Tell her I follow,
And the floods to the woods,
  Carry my holla, holla!
  Ce! la! ho! ho! hu!

(46)

ROBERT HERRICK.

A SWEET disorder in the dress
Kindles in clothes a wantonness :
A lawn about the shoulders thrown
Into a fine distraction :
An erring lace, which here and there
Enthralls the crimson stomacher :
A cuff neglectful, and thereby
Ribbands to flow confusedly :
A winning wave (deserving note)
In the tempestuous petticoat :
A careless shoe-string, in whose tie
I see a wild civility :
Do more bewitch me, than when art
Is too precise in every part.

(47)

ANONYMOUS.

YET if his majesty our sovereign lord
Should of his own accord
Friendly himself invite,
And say, 'I'll be your guest to-morrow night,'
How should we stir ourselves, call and command
All hands to work!   'Let no man idle stand.
Set me fine Spanish tables in the hall,
See they be fitted all;
Let there be room to eat,
And order taken that there want no meat.
See every sconce and candlestick made bright,
That without tapers they may give a light.
Look to the presence : are the carpets spread,
The dais o'er the head,
The cushions in the chairs,
And all the candles lighted on the stairs?
Perfume the chambers, and in any case
Let each man give attendance in his place.'

Thus if the king were coming, would we do,
And 'twere good reason too ;
For 'tis a duteous thing
To show all honour to an earthly king,
And after all our travail and our cost,
So he be pleased, to think no labour lost.
But at the coming of the King of Heaven,
All 's set at six and seven :
We wallow in our sin,
Christ cannot find a chamber in the inn.
We entertain Him always like a stranger,
And as at first still lodge Him in the manger.

(48)

JOHN FLETCHER.

HENCE, all you vain delights,
As short as are the nights
Wherein you spend your folly:
There 's nought in this life sweet
If man were wise to see 't,
But only melancholy,
O sweetest Melancholy!
Welcome folded arms and fixed eyes,
A sigh that piercing mortifies,
A look that 's fastened to the ground,
A tongue chain'd up without a sound!
Fountain heads, and pathless groves,
Places which pale passion loves!
Moonlight walks, when all the fowls
Are warmly housed, save bats and owls!
A midnight bell, a parting groan!
These are the sounds we feed upon;
Then stretch our bones in a still gloomy valley;
Nothing 's so dainty sweet as lovely melancholy.

(49)

THOMAS CAREW.

WHEN thou, poor excommunicate
    From all the joys of love, shalt see
The full reward, and glorious fate,
    Which my strong faith shall purchase me,
    Then curse thine own inconstancy.

A fairer hand than thine shall cure
    That heart which thy false oaths did wound;
And to my soul, a soul more pure
    Than thine shall by love's hand be bound,
    And both with equal glory crown'd.

Then shalt thou weep, entreat, complain
    To love, as I did once to thee;
When all thy tears shall be as vain
    As mine were then, for thou shalt be
    Damn'd for thy false apostasy.

(50)

JOHN FLETCHER.

'TIS late and cold; stir up the fire;
Sit close, and draw the table nigher;
Be merry, and drink wine that 's old,
A hearty medicine 'gainst a cold:
Your beds of wanton down the best,
Where you shall tumble to your rest;
I could wish you wenches too,
But I am dead, and cannot do.
Call for the best the house may ring,
Sack, white, and claret, let them bring,
And drink apace, while breath you have;
You 'll find but cold drink in the grave:
Plover, partridge, for your dinner,
And a capon for the sinner,
You shall find ready when you're up,
And your horse shall have his sup:
Welcome, welcome, shall fly round,
And I shall smile, though underground.

(51)

Thomas Heywood.

Pack, clouds, away, and welcome, day !
With night we banish sorrow.
Sweet air, blow soft ; mount, lark, aloft
To give my love good morrow.
Wings from the wind to please her mind,
Notes from the lark I'll borrow :
Bird, prime thy wing, nightingale, sing,
To give my love good morrow.
To give my love good morrow,
Notes from them all I 'll borrow.

Wake from thy nest, robin redbreast !
Sing, birds, in every furrow,
And from each bill let music shrill
Give my fair love good morrow.
Blackbird and thrush in every bush,
Stare, linnet, and cock-sparrow,
You pretty elves, among yourselves
Sing my fair love good morrow.
To give my love good morrow,
Sing, birds in every furrow.

(52)

THOMAS CAMPION.

SILLY boy! 'tis full moon yet, thy night as day shines
    clearly;
Had thy youth but wit to fear, thou couldst not love
    so dearly.
Shortly wilt thou mourn when all thy pleasures are
    bereavèd,
Little knows he how to love that never was deceivèd.

This is thy first maiden-flame that triumphs yet un-
    stainèd,
All is artless now you speak, not one word is feignèd;
All is heaven that you behold, and all your thoughts
    are blessèd,
But no spring can want his fall, each Troilus hath his
    Cressid.

Thy well-ordered locks ere long shall rudely hang
    neglected,

G

And thy lively pleasant cheer read grief on earth
    dejected ;
Much then wilt thou blame thy Saint, that made thy
    heart so holy
And with sighs confess, in love that too much faith is
    folly.

Yet be just and constant still, Love may beget a
    wonder,
Not unlike a summer's frost or fatal winter's thunder :
He that holds his sweetheart true unto his day of
    dying,
Lives, of all that ever breathed, most worthy the
    envying.

(53)

JAMES SHIRLEY.

THE glories of our blood and state
    Are shadows, not substantial things ;
There is no armour against fate ;
    Death lays his icy hand on kings :
        Sceptre and Crown
        Must tumble down,
And in the dust be equal made
With the poor crooked scythe and spade.

Some men with swords may reap the field,
    And plant fresh laurels where they kill :
But their strong nerves at last must yield ;
    They tame but one another still :
        Early or late
        They stoop to fate
And must give up their murmuring breath
When they, pale captives, creep to death.

The garlands wither on your brow;
  Then boast no more your mighty deeds;
Upon Death's purple altar now
  See where the victor-victim bleeds:
      Your heads must come
      To the cold tomb;
Only the actions of the just
Smell sweet, and blossom in their dust.

(54)

ROBERT HERRICK.

WHEN a daffodil I see,
Hanging down his head towards me ;
Guess I may, what I must be.
First, I shall decline my head ;
Secondly, I shall be dead ;
Lastly, safely burièd.

(55)

ROBERT JONES.

ONCE did my thoughts both ebb and flow,
    As passion did them move ;
Once did I hope, straight fear again,—
    And then I was in love.

Once did I waking spend the night,
    And tell how many minutes move.
Once did I wishing waste the day,—
    And then I was in love.

Once, by my carving true love's knot,
    The weeping trees did prove
That wounds and tears were both our lot,—
    And then I was in love.

Once did I breathe another's breath
    And in my mistress move,

Once was I not mine own at all,—
  And then I was in love.

Once I wore bracelets made of hair,
  And collars did approve,
Once wore my clothes made out of wax,—
  And then I was in love.

Once did I sonnet to my saint,
  My soul in numbers move,
Once did I tell a thousand lies,—
  And then I was in love.

Once in my ear did dangling hang
  A little turtle dove,
Once, in a word, I was a fool,—
  And then I was in love.

(56)

Thomas Carew.

Read in these roses the sad story
Of my hard fate and your own glory:
In the white you may discover
The paleness of a fainting lover;
In the red, the flames still feeding
On my heart with fresh wounds bleeding.
The white will tell you how I languish,
And the red express my anguish:
The white my innocence displaying,
The red my martyrdom betraying.
The frowns that on your brow resided,
Have those roses thus divided;
Oh ! let your smiles but clear the weather,
And then they both shall grow together.

(57)

ROBERT HERRICK.

GET up, get up for shame, the blooming morn
Upon her wings presents the god unshorn.
    See how Aurora throws her fair
    Fresh quilted colours through the air :
    Get up, sweet slug-a-bed, and see
    The dew bespangling herb and tree.
Each flower has wept, and bow'd toward the east,
Above an hour since ; yet you not drest,
    Nay ! not so much as out of bed ?
    When all the birds have Mattins said,
    And sung their thankful hymns : 'tis sin,
    Nay, profanation to keep in,
Whenas a thousand virgins on this day,
Spring, sooner than the lark, to fetch in May.

Rise ; and put on your foliage, and be seen
To come forth, like the Spring-time, fresh and green ;
    And sweet as Flora.   Take no care
    For jewels for your gown or hair :

Fear not ; the leaves will strew
Gems in abundance upon you :
Besides, the childhood of the day has kept,
Against you come, some orient pearls unwept :
    Come, and receive them while the light
    Hangs on the dewlocks of the night :
    And Titan on the eastern hill
    Retires himself, or else stands still
Till you come forth.   Wash, dress, be brief in praying :
Few beads are best when once we go a-Maying.

Come, my Corinna, come ; and coming, mark
How each field turns a street ; each street a park
    Made green, and trimmed with trees : see how
    Devotion gives each house a bough
    Or branch ; each porch, each door, ere this
    An ark, a tabernacle is
Made up of white-thorn neatly interwove ,
As if here were those cooler shades of love.
    Can such delights be in the street,
    And open fields, and we not see 't ?
    Come, we 'll abroad ; and let 's obey
    The proclamation made for May :
And sin no more, as we have done, by staying ;
But, my Corinna, come, let 's go a-Maying.

There 's not a budding boy or girl, this day,
But is got up, and gone to bring in May.

A deal of youth, ere this, is come
Back, and with white-thorn laden, home.
Some have despatched their cakes and cream,
Before that we have left to dream :
And some have wept, and wooed, and plighted troth,
And chose their priest, ere we can cast off sloth :
Many a green-gown has been given ;
Many a kiss, both odd and even :
Many a glance too has been sent
From out the eye Love's firmament :
Many a jest told of the key's betraying
This night, and locks picked, yet we 're not a-Maying.

Come, let us go, while we are in our prime ;
And take the harmless folly of the time
We shall grow old apace, and die
Before we know our liberty.
Our life is short ; and our days run
As fast away as does the sun :
And as a vapour, or a drop of rain
Once lost, can ne'er be found again :
So when you or I are made
A fable, song, or fleeting shade ;
All love, all liking, all delight
Lies drown'd with us in endless night.
Then while time serves, and we are but decaying :
Come, my Corinna, come, let 's go a-Maying.

(58)

JOHN WILSON.

GREEDY lover, pause awhile,
And remember that a smile
       Heretofore
Would have made thy hopes a feast ;
       Which is more
Since thy diet was increased,
Than both looks and language too,
Or the face itself, can do.

Such a province is my hand
As, if it thou couldst command
       Heretofore,
There thy lips would seem to dwell ;
       Which is more,
Ever since they sped so well,
Than they can be brought to do
By my neck and bosom too.

If the centre of my breast,
A dominion unpossessed
    Heretofore,
May thy wandering thoughts suffice,
    Seek no more,
And my heart shall be thy prize
So thou keep above the line,
All the hemisphere is thine.

If the flames of love were pure
Which by oath thou didst assure
    Heretofore,
Gold that goes into the clear
    Shines the more
When it leaves again the fire:
Let not then those looks of thine
Blemish what they should refine.

I have cast into the fire
Almost all thou couldst desire
    Heretofore;
But I see thou art to crave
    More and more.
Should I cast in all I have,
So that I were ne'er so free,
Thou wouldst burn, though not for me.

*is as very characteristic of it—
the variety, lightness of touch,
& happy turns of speech &c.   June 20. '13

I esp. underline the natural
almost colloquial little phrases.*

(59)

ROBERT JONES.

FAREWELL, dear love! since thou wilt needs be gone:
Mine eyes do show my life is almost done.
  —Nay I will never die,
  So long as I can spy;
  There be many mo
  Though that she do go.
There be many mo, I fear not;
Why, then, let her go, I care not.—

Farewell, farewell! since this I find is true,
I will not spend more time in wooing you.
  —But I will seek elsewhere
  If I may find her there.
  Shall I bid her go?
  What and if I do?
Shall I bid her go and spare not?
O no, no, no, no, I dare not.—

Ten thousand times farewell ! yet stay awhile.
Sweet, kiss me once, sweet kisses time beguile.
    —I have no power to move :
    How now, am I in love !—
    Wilt thou needs be gone ?
    Go then, all is one.
Wilt thou needs be gone ?   Oh, hie thee !
Nay ; stay, and do no more deny me.

Once more farewell ! I see *Loth to depart*
Bids oft adieu to her that holds my heart :
    But seeing I must lose
    Thy love which I did choose,
    Go thy ways for me,
    Since it may not be :
Go thy ways for me ! but whither ?
Go,—oh but where I may come thither.

What shall I do ? my love is now departed,
She is as fair as she is cruel-hearted :
    She would not be entreated
    With prayers oft repeated.
    If she come no more,
    Shall I die therefore ?
If she come no more, what care I ?
—Faith let her go, or come, or tarry !

(60)

JOHN FLETCHER

GOD LYÆUS, ever young,
Ever honoured, ever sung,
Stained with blood of lusty grapes,
In a thousand lusty shapes,
Dance upon the mazer's brim,
In the crimson liquor swim ;
From thy plenteous hand divine,
Let a river run with wine :
 God of youth, let this day here
 Enter neither care nor fear.

(61)

ROBERT JONES.

OFT have I mused the cause to find
   Why Love in ladies' eyes should dwell;
I thought, because himself was blind,
   He look'd that they should guide him well:
And sure his hope but seldom fails,
For Love by ladies' eyes prevails.

But time at last hath taught me wit,
   Although I bought my wit full dear;
For by her eyes my heart is hit,
   Deep is the wound though none appear:
Their glancing beams as darts he throws,
And sure he hath no shafts but those.

I mused to see their eyes so bright,
   And little thought they had been fire;
I gazed upon them with delight,
   But that delight hath bred desire:
What better place can Love desire
Than that where grows both shafts and fire?

(62)

SIR JOHN SUCKLING.

WHY so pale and wan, fond lover?
    Prithee why so pale?
Will, when looking well can't move her,
    Looking ill prevail?
    Prithee why so pale?

Why so dull and mute, young sinner?
    Prithee why so mute?
Will, when speaking well can't win her,
    Saying nothing do 't?
    Prithee why so mute?

Quit, quit, for shame; this will not move,
    This cannot take her;
If of herself she will not love,
    Nothing can make her:
    The devil take her!

(63)

THOMAS BATESON

SISTER, awake ! close not your eyes !
    The day her light discloses,
And the bright morning doth arise
    Out of her bed of roses.

See, the clear sun, the world's bright eye,
    In at our window peeping :
Lo ! how he blusheth to espy
    Us idle wenches sleeping.

Therefore, awake ! make haste, I say,
    And let us, without staying,
All in our gowns of green so gay
    Into the park a-Maying.

(64)

ROBERT HERRICK.

WELCOME, Maids of Honour,
    You do bring
    In the Spring;
And wait upon her.

She has Virgins many,
    Fresh and faire;
    Yet you are
More sweet than any.

Y' are the maiden posies,
    And so graced,
    To be placed
'Fore damask roses.

Yet though thus respected,
    By and by
    Ye do lie,
Poor girls, neglected.

(65)

SIR JOHN SUCKLING.

No, no, fair heretic, it needs must be
 But an ill love in me,
 And worse for thee;
For were it in my power
To love thee now this hour
 More than I did the last;
'Twould then so fall,
 I might not love at all;
Love that can flow, and can admit increase,
Admits as well an ebb, and may grow less.

True love is still the same; the torrid zones
 And those more frigid ones,
 It must not know:
For love grown cold or hot
 Is lust or friendship, not
 The thing we have.
For that's a flame would die,
Held down or up too high:
Then think I love more than I can express,
And would love more, could I but love thee less.

(66)

ROBERT HERRICK.

GATHER ye rosebuds while ye may,
    Old Time is still a-flying :
And this same flower that smiles to-day,
    To-morrow will be dying.

The glorious lamp of heaven, the sun,
    The higher he's a-getting ;
The sooner will his race be run,
    And nearer he's to setting.

That age is best, which is the first,
    When youth and blood are warmer ;
But being spent, the worse, and worst
    Times, still succeed the former.

Then be not coy, but use your time ;
    And while ye may go marry :
For having once but lost your prime,
    You may for ever tarry.

(67)

ANONYMOUS.

FAIN would I change that note
To which fond Love hath charmed me
Long long to sing by rote,
Fancying that that harmed me :
Yet when this thought did come
' Love is the perfect sum
      Of all delight,'
I have no other choice
Either for pen or voice
      To sing or write.

O Love ! they wrong thee much
That say thy sweet is bitter,
When thy rich fruit is such
As nothing can be sweeter.
Fair house of joy and bliss,
Where truest pleasure is,
      I do adore thee :
I know thee what thou art,
I serve thee with my heart,
      And fall before thee !

(68)

ROBERT HERRICK.

CHARM me asleep, and melt me so
    With thy delicious numbers ;
That being ravished, hence I go
    Away in easy slumbers.
        Ease my sick head,
        And make my bed,
    Thou power that canst sever
        From me this ill :
        And quickly still :
        Though thou not kill
            My fever.

Thou sweetly canst convert the same
    From a consuming fire,
Into a gently licking flame,
    And make it thus expire.
        Then make me weep
        My pains asleep ;

And give me such reposes,
  That I, poor I,
  May think, thereby,
  I live and die
    'Mongst roses.

Fall on me like a silent dew,
  Or like those maiden showers,
Which, by the peep of day, do strew
  A baptism o'er the flowers.
    Melt, melt my pains,
    With thy soft strains;
  That having ease me given,
    With full delight,
    I leave this light;
    And take my flight
      For Heaven.

(69)

THOMAS CAREW.

THE Lady Mary Villiers lies
Under this stone : with weeping eyes
The parents that first gave her birth,
And their sad friends, laid her in earth.
If any of them, reader, were
Known unto thee, shed a tear :
Or if thyself possess a gem,
As dear to thee as this to them ;
Though a stranger to this place,
Bewail in their's thine own hard case ;
For thou perhaps at thy return
Mayst find thy darling in an urn.

(70)

RICHARD BROME.

Nor Love nor Fate dare I accuse
For that my love did me refuse,
But oh! mine own unworthiness
That durst presume so mickle bliss
It was too much for me to love
A man so like the gods above:
An angel's shape, a saint-like voice,
Are too divine for human choice.

Oh had I wisely given my heart
For to have loved him but in part;
Sought only to enjoy his face,
Or any one peculiar grace
Of foot, of hand, of lip, or eye—
I might have lived where now I die:
But I, presuming all to chose,
Am now condemned all to lose.

(71)

Robert Herrick.

Come, sons of summer, by whose toil,
We are the lords of wine and oil:
By whose tough labours, and rough hands,
We rip up first, then reap our lands.
Crown'd with the ears of corn, now come,
And to the pipe, sing Harvest home.
Come forth, my lord, and see the cart
Dressed up with all the country art.
See, here a maukin, there a sheet,
As spotless pure, as it is sweet:
The horses, mares, and frisking fillies,
Clad, all, in linen, white as lilies.
The harvest swains, and wenches bound
For joy, to see the Hock-cart crown'd.
About the cart, hear, how the rout
Of rural younglings raise the shout;
Pressing before, some coming after,
Those with a shout, and these with laughter.
Some bless the cart; some kiss the sheaves;
Some prank them up with oaken leaves:

Some cross the fill-horse; some with great
Devotion, stroke the home-borne wheat :
While other rustics, less attent
To prayers, than to merriment,
Run after with their breeches rent.
Well, on, brave boys, to your lord's hearth,
Glitt'ring with fire; where, for your mirth,
Ye shall see first the large and chief
Foundation of your feast, fat beef :
With upper stories, mutton, veal,
And bacon, which makes full the meal,
With several dishes standing by,
As here a custard, there a pie,
And here all-tempting frumenty.
And for to make the merry cheer,
If smirking wine be wanting here,
There's that, which drowns all care, stout beer;
Which freely drink to your lord's health,
Then to the plough, (the common-wealth)
Next to your flails, your fanes, your fats;
Then to the maids with wheaten-hats :
To the rough sickle, and crooked scythe,
Drink, frolic, boys, till all be blythe.
Feed, and grow fat; and as ye eat,
Be mindful, that the labouring neat,
As you, may have their fill of meat.
And know, besides, ye must revoke
The patient ox unto the yoke,

All all go back unto the plough
And harrow, though they 're hanged up now.
And, you must know, your lord's word 's true,
Feed him ye must, whose food fills you.
And that this pleasure is like rain,
Not sent ye for to drown your pain,
But for to make it spring again.

(72)

RICHARD BROME.

Come, come away! the spring,
By every bird that can but sing,
Or chirp a note, doth now invite
Us forth to taste of his delight,
In field, in grove, on hill, in dale ;
But above all the nightingale,
Who in her sweetness strives t' outdo
The loudness of the hoarse cuckoo.
 'Cuckoo,' cries he ; 'Jug, jug, jug,' sings she ;
 From bush to bush, from tree to tree :
 Why in one place then tarry we?

Come away! why do we stay?
We have no debt or rent to pay ;
No bargains or accounts to make,
Nor land or lease to let or take :
Or if we had, should that remore us
When all the world 's our own before us,
And where we pass and make resort,
It is our kingdom and our court.
 'Cuckoo,' cries he ; 'Jug, jug, jug,' sings she ;
 From bush to bush, from tree to tree :
 Why in one place then tarry we?

(73)

THOMAS CAMPION.

THERE is a garden in her face
Where roses and white lilies grow ;
A heavenly paradise is that place
Wherein all pleasant fruits doth flow.
  There cherries grow which none may buy,
  Till 'Cherry ripe' themselves do cry.

These cherries fairly do enclose
Of orient pearl a double row,
Which when her lovely laughter shows,
They look like rosebuds filled with snow ;
  Yet them nor peer nor prince can buy,
  Till 'Cherry ripe' themselves do cry.

Her eyes like angels watch them still,
Her brows like bended bows do stand,
Threatening with piercing frowns to kill
All that attempt with eye or hand
  Those sacred cherries to come nigh
  Till 'Cherry ripe' themselves do cry.

(74)

Sir William Davenant.

WAKE all the dead! what ho! what ho!
How soundly sleep they whose pillows lie low!
They mind not poor lovers who walk above
On the decks of the world in storms of love.
No whisper now nor glance shall pass
Through wickets or through panes of glass;
For our windows and doors are shut and barred.
Lie close in the church, and in the churchyard.
In every grave make room, make room!
The world's at an end, and we come, we come.

The state is now love's foe, love's foe;
'T has seized on his arms, his quiver and bow;
Has pinioned his wings, and fettered his feet,
Because he made way for lovers to meet.
But, O sad chance, his judge was old;
Hearts cruel grow, when blood grows cold.
No man being young his process would draw.
O heavens, that love should be subject to law!
Lovers go woo the dead, the dead!
Lie two in a grave, and to bed, to bed!

(75)

THOMAS FORD.

THERE is a Lady sweet and kind,
Was never face so pleased my mind;
I did but see her passing by,
And yet I love her till I die.

Her gesture, motion, and her smiles,
Her wit, her voice my heart beguiles,
Beguiles my heart, I know not why,
And yet I love her till I die.

Her free behaviour, winning looks
Will make a lawyer burn his books;
I touch'd her not, alas! not I.
And yet I love her till I die.

Had I her fast betwixt mine arms,
Judge you that think such sports were harms;
Were 't any harm? no, no, fie, fie,
For I will love her till I die.

Should I remain confinèd there
So long as Phoebus in his sphere,
I to request, she to deny,
Yet would I love her till I die.

Cupid is wingèd and doth range,
Her country so my love doth change:
But change she earth, or change she sky,
Yet will I love her till I die.

(76)

ROBERT HERRICK.

WHY do ye weep, sweet babes? can tears
        Speak grief in you,
        Who were but born
    Just as the modest morn
    Teemed her refreshing dew?
Alas, you have not known that shower,
        That mars a flower;
        Nor felt th' unkind
    Breath of a blasting wind;
    Nor are ye worn with years;
        Or warped as we,
    Who think it strange to see,
Such pretty flowers, like to orphans young,
To speak by tears, before ye have a tongue.

Speak, whimp'ring younglings, and make known
        The reason, why
        Ye droop, and weep;

Is it for want of sleep?
Or childish lullaby?
Or that ye have not seen as yet
    The violet?
    Or brought a kiss
From that sweetheart, to this?
No, no, this sorrow shown
    By your tears shed,
Would have this lecture read,
That things of greatest, so of meanest worth,
Conceived with care are, and with tears brought
    forth.

(77)

ANONYMOUS.

WHY should I wrong my judgment so,
As for to love where I do know
    There is no hold for to be taken?

For what her wish thirsts after most,
If once of it her heart can boast,
    Straight by her folly 'tis forsaken.

Thus whilst I still pursue in vain,
Methinks I turn a child again,
    And of my shadow am a-chasing.

For all her favours are to me
Like apparitions which I see,
    But never can come near th' embracing.

Oft had I wished that there had been
Some almanack whereby to have seen,
    When love with her had been in season.

But I perceive there is no art
Can find the epact of the heart,
    That loves by chance, and not by reason.

Yet will I not for this despair,
For time her humour may prepare
    To grace him who is now neglected.

And what unto my constancy
She now denies, one day may be
    From her inconstancy expected.

(78)

RICHARD LOVELACE.

TELL me not, sweet, I am unkind
    That from the nunnery
Of thy chaste breast and quiet mind,
    To war and arms I fly.

True, a new mistress now I chase,
    The first foe in the field ;
And with a stronger faith embrace
    A sword, a horse, a shield.

Yet this inconstancy is such
    As you too shall adore ;
I could not love thee, Dear, so much,
    Loved I not Honour more.

(79)

Jones or Campion (?)

Though your strangeness frets my heart,
    Yet must I not complain ;
You persuade me 'tis but art
    Which secret love must feign ;
If another you affect,
'Tis but a toy t' avoid suspect.
Is this fair excusing ?
O no, all is abusing.

When your wish'd sight I desire,
    Suspicion you pretend,
Causeless you yourself retire
    Whilst I in vain attend,
Thus a lover, as you say,
Still made more eager by delay
Is this fair excusing ?
O no, all is abusing

When another holds your hand,
    You 'll swear I hold your heart ;
Whilst my rival close doth stand
    And I sit far apart,
I am nearer yet than they,
Hid in your bosom, as you say.
Is this fair excusing ?
O no, all is abusing.

Would a rival then I were
    Or else a secret friend,
So much lesser should I fear
    And not so much attend.
They enjoy you, every one,
Yet must I seem your friend alone.
Is this fair excusing ?
O no, all is abusing.

(80)

ROBERT HERRICK.

BID me to live, and I will live
  Thy protestant to be :
Or bid me love, and I will give
  A loving heart to thee.

A heart as soft, a heart as kind,
  A heart as sound and free,
As in the whole world thou canst find,
  That heart I 'll give to thee.

Bid that heart stay and it will stay,
  To honour thy decree :
Or bid it languish quite away,
  And 't shall do so for thee.

Bid me to weep, and I will weep,
  While I have eyes to see :

And having none, yet I will keep
A heart to weep for thee.

Bid me despair, and I 'll despair,
Under that cypress tree :
Or bid me die, and I will dare
E'en death, to die for thee.

Thou art my life, my love, my heart
The very eyes of me :
And hast command of every part
To live and die for thee.

(81)

THOMAS CAMPION.

TURN all thy thoughts to eyes,
Turn all thy hairs to ears,
Change all thy friends to spies,
And all thy joys to fears ;
　　True love will yet be free
　　In spite of jealousy.

Turn darkness into day,
Conjectures into truth,
Believe what th' envious say,
Let age interpret youth :
　　True love will yet be free
　　In spite of jealousy.

Wrest every word and look,
Rack every hidden thought ;
Or fish with golden hook,
True love cannot be caught :
　　For that will still be free
　　In spite of jealousy

(82)

THOMAS CAREW.

GIVE me more love, or more disdain,
  The torrid, or the frozen zone
Bring equal ease unto my pain ;
  The temperate affords me none :
Either extreme, of love or hate,
Is sweeter than a calm estate.

Give me a storm ; if it be love,
  Like Danae in that golden shower,
I swim in pleasure ; if it prove
  Disdain, that torrent will devour
My vulture-hopes ; and he 's possess'd
Of Heaven that 's but from Hell releas'd :
Then crown my joys, or cure my pain ;
Give me more love, or more disdain.

(83)

RICHARD LOVELACE.

WHEN Love with unconfinèd wings
  Hovers within my gates,
And my divine Althea brings
  To whisper at the grates;
When I lie tangled in her hair
  And fettered to her eye,
The birds that wanton in the air
  Know no such liberty.

When flowing cups run swiftly round
  With no allaying Thames,
Our careless heads with roses crowned,
  Our hearts with loyal flames;
When thirsty grief in wine we steep,
  When healths and draughts go free—
Fishes that tipple in the deep
  Know no such liberty.

When linnet-like confinèd, I
   With shriller throat shall sing
The sweetness, mercy, majesty,
   And glories of my King;
When I shall voice aloud how good
   He is, how great should be,
Enlargèd winds, that curl the flood,
   Know no such liberty.

Stone walls do not a prison make,
   Nor iron bars a cage;
Minds innocent and quiet take
   That for an hermitage:
If I have freedom in my love
   And in my soul am free,
Angels alone, that soar above,
   Enjoy such liberty.

(84)

JOHN DOWLAND.

WHAT poor astronomers are they,
Take women's eyes for stars!
And set their thoughts in battle 'ray,
To fight such idle wars;
When in the end they shall approve,
'Tis but a jest drawn out of Love.

And Love itself is but a jest
Devised by idle heads,
To catch young fancies in the nest,
And lay them in fools' beds;
That being hatched in beauty's eyes
They may be fledged e'er they be wise.

But yet it is a sport to see,
How Wit will run on wheels!
While wit cannot persuaded be,
With that which reason feels,
That women's eyes and stars are odd,
And Love is but a feignèd god!

K

But such as will run mad with Will,
I cannot clear their sight,
But leave them to their study still,
To look where is no light !
Till time too late, we make them try,
They study false Astronomy.

(85)

THOMAS CAREW.

Ask me no more where Jove bestows,
When June is past, the fading rose ;
For in your beauties, orient deep,
These flow'rs, as in their causes, sleep.

Ask me no more, whither do stray
The golden atoms of the day ;
For, in pure love, Heaven did prepare
Those powders to enrich your hair.

Ask me no more, whither doth haste
The nightingale, when May is past ;
For in your sweet dividing throat
She winters, and keeps warm her note.

Ask me no more, where those stars light,
That downwards fall in dead of night ;
For in your eyes they sit, and there
Fixed become, as in their sphere.

Ask me no more, if east or west,
The phœnix builds her spicy nest ;
For unto you at last she flies,
And in your fragrant bosom dies.

(86)

THOMAS CAMPION.

WHETHER men do laugh or weep,
Whether they do wake or sleep,
Whether they die young or old,
Whether they feel heat or cold;
There is underneath the sun
Nothing in true earnest done.

All our pride is but a jest,
None are worst and none are best;
Grief and joy and hope and fear
Play their pageants everywhere:
Vain Opinion all doth sway,
And the world is but a play.

Powers above in clouds do sit,
Mocking our poor apish wit,
That so lamely with such state
Their high glory imitate.
No ill can be felt but pain,
And that happy men disdain.

(87)

ROBERT HERRICK.

FAIR daffodils, we weep to see
        You haste away so soon :
As yet the early rising sun
        Has not attained his noon.
            Stay, stay,
        Until the hasting day
                Has run
        But to the Even-song ;
And, having prayed together, we
            Will go with you along.

We have short time to stay, as you
        We have as short a spring ;
As quick a growth to meet decay
        As you, or any thing.
            We die,
        As your hours do, and dry
                Away,
        Like to the summer's rain ;
Or as the pearls of morning's dew
            Ne'er to be found again.

(88)

RICHARD LOVELACE.

OH thou, that swing'st upon the waving ear
  Of some well-filled oaten beard,
Drunk ev'ry night with a delicious tear
  Dropped thee from heaven where now thou'rt
    reared !

The joys of earth and air are thine entire,
  That with thy feet and wings dost hop and fly ;
And when thy poppy works, thou dost retire
  To thy carved acorn-bed to lie.

Up with the sun, the day thou welcom'st then,
  Sport'st in the gilt plats of his beams,
And all these merry days mak'st merry men,
  Thyself and melancholy streams.

But ah, the sickle !   Golden ears. are cropped ;
  Ceres and Bacchus bid good-night ;
Sharp frosty fingers all your flowers have topped,
  And what scythes spared, winds shave off quite.

Poor verdant fool! and now green ice, thy joys
   Large and as lasting as thy perch of grass,
Bid us lay in 'gainst winter rain, and poise
   Their floods with an o'erflowing glass.

Thou best of men and friends! we will create
   A genuine summer in each other's breast;
And spite of this cold time and frozen fate,
   Thaw us a warm seat to our rest.

Our sacred hearths shall burn eternally
   As vestal flames; the North-wind, he
Shall strike his frost-stretched wings, dissolve and fly
   This Etna in epitome.

Dropping December shall come weeping in,
   Bewail th' usurping of his reign;
But when in showers of old Greek we begin,
   Shall cry, he hath his crown again!

Night as clear Hesper shall our tapers whip
   From the light casements, where we play,
And the dark hag from her black mantle strip,
   And stick there everlasting day.

'Thus richer than untempted kings are we,
   That asking nothing, nothing need:
Though lord of all what seas embrace, yet he
   That wants himself, is poor indeed.

(89)

GEORGE HERBERT.

LORD, who createdst man in wealth and store,
  Though foolishly he lost the same,
      Decaying more and more,
          Till he became
              Most poor:

              With Thee
          O let me rise,
      As larks, harmoniously,
  And sing this day Thy victories:
Then shall the fall further the flight in me.

My tender age in sorrow did begin;
  And still with sicknesses and shame
      Thou didst so punish sin,
          That I became
              Most thin.

              With Thee
          Let me combine,
      And feel this day Thy victory;
  For if I imp my wing on Thine,
Affliction shall advance the flight in me.

(90)

THOMAS CAREW.

In Love's name, you are charg'd hereby,
To make a speedy hue and cry
After a face which t'other day,
Stole my wand'ring heart away.
To direct you, these, in brief,
Are ready marks to know the thief.
　　Her hair a net of beams would prove,
Strong enough to capture Jove
In his eagle shape; her brow
Is a comely field of snow;
Her eye so rich, so pure a gray
Every beam creates a day;
And if she but sleep (not when
The Sun sets) 'tis night again;
In her cheeks are to be seen
Of flowers both the king and queen,
Thither by the graces led,
And freshly laid in nuptial bed;
On whose lips like nymphs do wait,
Who deplore their virgin state;

Oft they blush, and blush for this,
That they one another kiss :
But observe, besides the rest,
You shall know this felon best
By her tongue ; for if your ear
Once a heavenly music hear,
Such as neither gods nor men,
But from that voice, shall hear again,
That, that is she.   O straight surprise,
And bring her unto Love's assize :
If you let her go, she may
Antedate the latter day,
Fate and philosophy control,
And leave the world without a soul.

(91)

THOMAS CAMPION.

YOUNG and simple though I am
I have heard of Cupid's name,
Guess I can what thing it is
Men desire when they do kiss:
    Smoke can never burn, they say,
    But the flames that follow may.

I am not so foul or fair
To be proud or to despair;
Yet my lips have oft observed
Men that kiss them press them hard,
    As glad lovers use to do
    When their new-met loves they woo.

Faith, 'tis but a foolish mind,
Yet methinks a heat I find
Like thirst-longing, that doth bide
Ever on my weaker side,
    Where they say my heart doth move:
    Venus grant it be not love!

If it be, alas !   What then ?
Were not women made for men ?
And good 'tis a thing were past,
That must needs be done at last :
      Roses that are overblown
      Grow less sweet, then fall alone.

Yet nor churl nor silken gull
Shall my maiden blossom pull,
Who shall not I soon can tell,
Who shall would I could as well :
      This I know, whoe'er he be,
      Love he must, or flatter me.

(92)

SIR JOHN SUCKLING.

'Tis now since I sat down before
  That foolish fort, a heart;
(Time strangely spent) a year or more,
  And still I did my part:

Made my approaches, from her hand
  Unto her lip did rise,
And did already understand
  The language of her eyes.

Proceeded on with no less art—
  My tongue was engineer—
I thought to undermine the heart
  By whispering in the ear.

When this did nothing, I brought down
  Great cannon-oaths and shot
A thousand thousand to the town,
  And still it yielded not.

I then resolved to starve the place
    By cutting off all kisses,
Praying, and gazing on her face,
    And all such little blisses.

To draw her out, and from her strength
    I drew all batteries in :
And brought myself to lie at length,
    As if no siege had been.

When I had done what man could do,
    And thought the place mine own,
The enemy lay quiet too,
    And smiled at all was done.

I sent to know from whence and where
    These hopes and this relief?
A spy informed, Honour was there,
    And did command in chief.

March, march, quoth I, the word straight give,
    Let 's lose no time, but leave her ;
That giant upon air will live,
    And hold it out for ever.

To such a place our camp remove,
    As will no siege abide ;
I hate a fool that starves her love,
    Only to feed her pride.

(93)

George Herbert.

Lord, in my silence how do I despise
  What upon trust
Is styled honour, riches, or fair eyes,
  But is fair dust!
 I surname them gilded clay,
 Dear earth, fine grass or hay;
In all, I think my foot doth ever tread
  Upon their head.

But when I view abroad both regiments,
  The world's and thine,—
Thine clad with simpleness and sad events;
  The other fine,
 Full of glory and gay weeds,
 Brave language, braver deeds,—
That which was dust before doth quickly rise,
  And prick mine eyes.

O, brook not this, lest if what even now
My foot did tread
Affront those joys wherewith Thou didst endow
And long since wed
My poor soul, even sick of love,—
It may a Babel prove,
Commodious to conquer heaven and Thee,
Planted in me.

(94)

SIR JOHN SUCKLING.

OUT upon it, I have loved
  Three whole days together ;
And am like to love three more,
  If it prove fair weather.

Time shall moult away his wings,
  Ere he shall discover
In the whole wide world again
  Such a constant lover.

But the spite on 't is, no praise
  Is due at all to me :
Love with me had made no stays,
  Had it any been but she,

Had it any been but she,
  And that very face,
There had been at least ere this
  A dozen dozen in her place.

(95)

THOMAS CAMPION (?)

WHEN to her lute Corinna sings,
Her voice revives the leaden strings,
And doth in highest notes appear
As any challenged echo clear :
But when she doth of mourning speak,
E'en with her sighs the strings do break.
And as her lute doth live or die,
Led by her passion, so must I :
For when of pleasure she doth sing,
My thoughts enjoy a sudden spring ;
But if she doth of sorrow speak,
E'en from my heart the strings do break.

(96)

GEORGE HERBERT.

SWEET day, so cool, so calm, so bright,
The bridal of the earth and sky,
The dew shall weep thy fall to-night;
       For thou must die.

Sweet rose, whose hue angry and brave
Bids the rash gazer wipe his eye,
Thy root is ever in its grave,—
       And thou must die.

Sweet spring, full of sweet days and roses,
A box where sweets compacted lie,
My music shows ye have your closes,
       And all must die.

Only a sweet and virtuous soul,
Like seasoned timber, never gives;
But though the whole world turn to coal,
       Then chiefly lives.

(97)

MARQUESS OF MONTROSE.

My dear and only love, I pray
   That little world of thee
Be governed by no other sway
   Than purest monarchy ;
For if confusion have a part,
   Which virtuous souls abhor,
And hold a synod in thy heart,
   I 'll never love thee more.

As Alexander I will reign,
   And I will reign alone ;
My thoughts did evermore disdain
   A rival on my throne.
He either fears his fate too much,
   Or his deserts are small,
That dares not put it to the touch,
   To gain or lose it all.

But I will reign and govern still,
  And always give the law,
And have each subject at my will,
  And all to stand in awe;
But 'gainst my batteries if I find
  Thou kick, or vex me sore,
As that thou set me up a blind,
  I 'll never love thee more.

And in the empire of thine heart,
  Where I should solely be,
If others do pretend a part,
  Or dare to vie with me,
Or if committees thou erect,
  And go on such a score,
I 'll laugh and sing at thy neglect,
  And never love thee more.

But if thou wilt prove faithful, then,
  And constant of thy word,
I 'll make thee glorious by my pen,
  And famous by my sword;
I 'll serve thee in such noble ways
  Was never heard before;
I 'll crown and deck thee all with bays,
  And love thee more and more.

(98)

SIR JOHN SUCKLING.

I PRITHEE spare me, gentle boy,
Press me no more for that slight toy,
That foolish trifle of an heart;
I swear it will not do its part,
Though thou dost thine, employ'st thy power
  and art.

For through long custom it has known
The little secrets, and is grown
Sullen and wise, will have its will,
And, like old hawks, pursues that still
That makes least sport, flies only where 't can
  kill.

Some youth that has not made his story,
Will think, perchance, the pain 's the glory;
And mannerly fit out love's feast;
I shall be carving of the best,
Rudely call for the last course 'fore the rest.

And, O, when once that course is past,
How short a time the feast doth last!
Men rise away, and scarce say grace,
Or civilly once thank the face
That did invite; but seek another place.

(99)

THOMAS MORLEY.

MISTRESS mine, well may you fare !
Kind be your thoughts and void of care,
Sweet Saint Venus be your speed
That you may in love proceed.
Coll me and clip, and kiss me too,
So so so so so so true love should do.

This fair morning, sunny bright,
That give's life to love's delight,
Every heart with heat inflames,
And our cold affection blames.
Coll me and clip, and kiss me too,
So so so so so so true love should do.

In these woods are none but birds,
They can speak but silent words ;
They are pretty harmless things,
They will shade us with their wings.
Coll me and clip, and kiss me too,
So so so so so so true love should do.

Never strive nor make no noise,
'Tis for foolish girls and boys ;
Every childish thing can say
' Go to, how now, pray away ! '
Coll me and clip, and kiss me too,
So so so so so so true love should do.

(100)

GEORGE HERBERT.

THE merry World did on a day
With his train-bands and mates agree
To meet together where I lay,
And all in sport to jeer at me.

First Beauty crept into a rose,
Which when I pluckt not, 'Sir,' said she,
'Tell me, I pray, whose hands are those?'
But Thou shalt answer, Lord, for me.

Then Money came, and chinking still,
'What tune is this, poor man?' said he;
'I heard in music you had skill:'
But Thou shalt answer, Lord, for me.

Then came brave Glory, puffing by
In silks that whistled, who but he!
He scarce allowed me half an eye:
But Thou shalt answer, Lord, for me.

Then came quick Wit and Conversation,
And he would needs a comfort be,
And, to be short, make an oration :
But Thou shalt answer, Lord, for me.

Yet when the hour of Thy design
To answer these five things shall come,
Speak not at large, say, I am Thine,
And then they have their answer home.

(101)

SIR JOHN SUCKLING.

My dearest rival, lest our love
Should with eccentric motion move,
Before it learn to go astray,
We 'll teach and set it in a way,
And such directions give unto 't,
That it shall never wander foot.
Know first, then, we will serve as true
For one poor smile, as we would do,
If we had what our higher flame,
Or our vainer wish could frame.
Impossible shall be our hope ;
And love shall only have his scope
To join with fancy now and then,
And think what reason would condemn :
And on these grounds we 'll love as true,
As if they were most sure t' ensue :
And chastly for these things we 'll stay,
As if to-morrow were the day.
Meantime we two will teach our hearts
In love's-burdens bear their parts :

Thou first shall sigh, and say She 's fair ;
And I 'll still answer, Past compare.
Thou shalt set out each part o' th' face,
While I extol each little grace ;
Thou shalt be ravished at her wit ;
And I, that she so governs it :
Thou shalt like well that hand, that eye,
That lip, that look, that majesty ;
And in good language them adore :
While I want words and do it more.
Yea we will sit and sigh awhile,
And with soft thoughts some time beguile ;
But straight again break out, and praise
All we had done before, new ways.
Thus will we do till paler death
Come with a warrant for our breath,
And then whose fate shall be to die,
First of us two, by legacy
Shall all his store bequeath, and give
His love to him that shall survive ;
For no one stock can ever serve
To love so much as she 'll deserve.

(102)

THOMAS CAMPION.

VIEW me, Lord, a work of Thine !
   Shall I then lie drowned in night ?
Might Thy grace in me but shine,
   I should seem made all of light.

But my soul still surfeits so
   On the poisoned baits of sin,
That I strange and ugly grow ;
   All is dark and foul within.

Cleanse me, Lord, that I may kneel
   At Thine altar pure and white ;
They that once Thy mercies feel,
   Gaze no more on earth's delight.

Worldly joys like shadows fade
   When the heavenly light appears :
But the covenants Thou hast made,
   Endless, know nor days nor years.

In Thy Word, Lord, is my trust,
   To Thy mercies fast I fly ;
Though I am but clay and dust,
   Yet Thy grace can lift me high.

(103)

ANDREW MARVELL.

WHEN for the thorns with which I long, too long,
    With many a piercing wound,
    My Saviour's head have crown'd,
I seek with garlands to redress that wrong:
    Through every garden, every mead,
I gather flowers—(my fruits are only flowers),
    Dismantling all the fragrant towers
That once adorn'd my shepherdess's head:
And now, when I have summ'd up all my store,
    Thinking (so I myself deceive),
    So rich a chaplet thence to weave
As never yet the King of Glory wore:
    Alas! I find the Serpent old,
    That, twining in his speckled breast,
    About the flowers disguised does fold
    With wreaths of fame and interest.
Ah, foolish man, that would'st debase with them,
And mortal glory, Heaven's diadem!
But Thou who only could'st the Serpent tame,
Either his slippery knots at once untie,

And disentangle all his winding snare;
Or shatter too, with him, my curious frame,
And let these wither—so that he may die—
Though set with skill, and chosen out with care:
That they while Thou on both their spoils dost
    tread,
May crown Thy feet, that could not crown Thy
    head.

(104)

THOMAS WEELKES.

THREE times a day my prayer is
To gaze my fill on Thoralis,
And three times thrice I daily pray
Not to offend that sacred may;
But all the year my suit must be
That I may please and she love me.

(105)

SIR JOHN SUCKLING.

HONEST lover whatsoever,
If in all thy love there ever
Was one wav'ring thought, if thy flame
Were not still even, still the same :
      Know this,
    Thou lov'st amiss,
    And to love true,
Thou must begin again and love anew

If when she appears i' th' room,
Thou dost not quake, and art struck dumb,
And in striving this to cover,
Dost not speak thy words twice over,
      Know this,
    Thou lov'st amiss,
    And to love true,
Thou must begin again, and love anew.

If fondly thou dost not mistake,
And all defects for graces take,
Persuad'st thyself that jests are broken,
When she hath little or nothing spoken,
          Know this,
        Thou lov'st amiss,
        And to love true,
Thou must begin again, and love anew.

If when thou appear'st to be within,
And lett'st not men ask and ask again ;
And when thou answerest, if it be,
To what was asked thee, properly,
          Know this,
        Thou lov'st amiss,
        And to love true,
Thou must begin again, and love anew.

If when thy stomach calls to eat,
Thou cutt'st not fingers 'stead of meat,
And with much gazing on her face
Dost not rise hungry from the place,
          Know this,
        Thou lov'st amiss,
        And to love true,
Thou must begin again, and love anew.

If by this thou dost discover
That thou art no perfect lover,
And desiring to love true,
Thou dost begin to love anew :
Know this,
Thou lov'st amiss,
And to love true,
Thou must begin again, and love anew.

(106)

ROBERT HERRICK.

GOOD-MORROW to the day so fair;
  Good morning, sir, to you:
Good-morrow to mine own torn hair
  Bedabbled with the dew.

Good morning to this primrose too;
  Good-morrow to each maid;
That will with flowers the tomb bestrew,
  Wherein my love is laid.

Ah! woe is me, woe, woe is me
  Alack and welladay!
For pity, sir, find out that bee,
  Which bore my love away.

I 'll seek him in your bonnet brave;
  I 'll seek him in your eyes;
Nay, now I think they 've made his grave
  I' the bed of strawberries.

I 'll seek him there ; I know, ere this,
   The cold, cold earth doth shake him ;
But I will go, or send a kiss
   By you, sir, to awake him.

Pray hurt him not ; though he be dead,
   He knows well who do love him,
And who with green turfs rear his head,
   And who do rudely move him.

He 's soft and tender : pray take heed :
   With bands of cowslips bind him ;
And bring him home ; but 'tis decreed,
   That I shall never find him.

(107)

GEORGE HERBERT.

A BROKEN Altar, Lord, Thy servant rears,
Made of a heart, and cemented with tears,
    Whose parts are as Thy hand did frame ;
    No workman's tool hath touched the same.
        A heart alone
        Is such a stone,
        As nothing but
        Thy power doth cut.
        Wherefore each part
        Of my hard heart
        Meets in this frame,
        To praise Thy name :
    That if I chance to hold my peace
    These stones to praise Thee may not cease.
O, let Thy blessed Sacrifice be mine,
And sanctify this Altar to be Thine !

(108)

HENRY VAUGHAN.

CAN any tell me what it is ?   Can you,
  That wind your thoughts into a clue,
To guide out others, while yourselves stay in,
      And hug the sin ?
I who so long in it have lived,
      That, if I might,
In truth I would not be reprieved,
      Have neither sight
      Nor sense that knows
      These ebbs and flows.
But since of all, all may be said,
And likeliness doth but upbraid
And mock the truth which still is lost
In fine conceits, like streams in a sharp frost ;
  I will not strive, nor the rule break,
  Which doth give losers leave to speak.
Then false and foul world, and unknown
      Even to thy own,
Here I renounce thee, and resign
Whatever thou canst say is thine.

Thou art not Truth! for he that tries
Shall find thee all deceit and lies.
Thou art not Friendship! for in thee
'Tis but the bait of policy;
Which like a viper lodged in flowers,
Its venom through that sweetness pours.
And when not so, then always 'tis
A fading paint, the short-lived bliss
Of air and humour, out and in,
Like colours in a dolphin's skin:
But must not live beyond one day,
Or for convenience, then away.
Thou art not Riches! for that trash,
Which one age hoards, the next doth wash,
And so severely sweep away,
That few remember where it lay.
So rapid streams the wealthy land
About them have at their command;
And shifting channels here restore,
There break down, what they banked before.
Thou art not Honour! for those gay
Feathers will wear and drop away;
And princes to some upstart line
Give new ones, that are full as fine.
Thou art not Pleasure! for thy rose
Upon a thorn doth still repose,
Which, if not dropped, will quickly shed,
But soon as cropped grows dull and dead.

Thou art the sand which fills one glass,
And then doth to another pass;
And could I put thee to a stay,
Thou art but dust.   Then go thy way,
And leave me clean and bright, though poor;
Who stops thee doth but daub his floor;
And, swallow-like, when he hath done,
To unknown dwellings must be gone.

Welcome pure thoughts and peaceful hours,
Enriched with sunshine and with showers!
Welcome fair hopes and holy cares,
The not-to-be-repented shares
Of time and business, the sure road
Unto my last and loved abode!
     O supreme bliss!
The circle, centre, and abyss
Of blessings, never let me miss
Nor leave that path, which leads to Thee,
Who art alone all things to me!
I hear, I see, all the long day
The noise and pomp of the 'broad way;'
I note their coarse and proud approaches,
Their silks, perfumes, and glittering coaches.
But in the 'narrow way' to Thee
I observe only poverty,
And despised things; and all along
The ragged, mean, and humble throng

Are still on foot ; and as they go
They sigh, and say their Lord went so !

Give me my staff then, as it stood
When green and growing in the wood.
(Those stones, which for the altar served,
Might not be smoothed nor finely carved :)
With this poor stick, I 'll pass the ford,
As Jacob did.   And Thy dear word,
As Thou hast dressed it, not as wit
And depraved tastes have poisoned it,
Shall in the passage be my meat,
And none else will Thy servant eat.
Thus, thus, and in no other sort,
Will I set forth, though laughed at for 't ;
And leaving the wise world their way,
Go through, though judged to go astray.

(109)

ROBERT HERRICK.

HER eyes the glow-worm lend thee,
The shooting stars attend thee ;
    And the elves also,
    Whose little eyes glow,
Like the sparks of fire, befriend thee.

No Will-o-the-Wisp mislight thee ;
Nor snake, or slow-worm bite thee ;
    But on, on thy way,
    Not making a stay,
Since ghost there 's none to affright thee.

Let not the dark thee cumber ;
What though the moon does slumber ;
    The stars of the night
    Will lend thee their light,
Like tapers clear without number.

Then Julia, let me woo thee,
Thus, thus to come unto me :
    And when I shall meet
    Thy silv'ry feet,
My soul I 'll pour into thee.

(110)

John Fletcher

Drink to-day, and drown all sorrow,
You shall perhaps not do it to-morrow :
Best, while you have it, use your breath ;
There is no drinking after death.

Wine works the heart up, wakes the wit,
There is no cure 'gainst age but it :
It helps the head-ache, cough, and ptisick,
And is for all diseases physic.

Then let us swill, boys, for our health ;
Who drinks well, loves the commonwealth.
And he that will to bed go sober
Falls with the leaf, still in October.

(111)

HENRY VAUGHAN.

HAPPY those early days, when I
Shined in my angel-infancy!
Before I understood this place
Appointed for my second race,
Or taught my soul to fancy ought
But a white celestial thought;
When yet I had not walked above
A mile or two from my first Love,
And looking back, at that short space,
Could see a glimpse of his bright face;
When on some gilded cloud or flower
My gazing soul would dwell an hour,
And in those weaker glories spy
Some shadows of eternity;
Before I taught my tongue to wound
My conscience with a sinful sound,
Or had the black art to dispense
A several sin to every sense,

But felt through all this fleshly dress
Bright shoots of everlastingness.
　　O how I long to travel back,
And tread again that ancient track !
That I might once more reach that plain,
Where first I left my glorious train ;
From whence th' enlightened spirit sees
That shady City of Palm trees.
But ah ! my soul with too much stay
Is drunk, and staggers in the way !
Some men a forward motion love,
But I by backward steps would move ;
And, when this dust falls to the urn,
In that state I came, return.

(112)

WILLIAM HABINGTON.

Nox nocti indicat scientiam.

WHEN I survey the bright
　　Celestial sphere :
So rich with jewels hung, that night
Doth like an Ethiop bride appear :

My soul her wings doth spread,
　　And heavenward flies,
The Almighty's mysteries to read
In the large volume of the skies.

For the bright firmament
　　Shoots forth no flame
So silent, but is eloquent
In speaking the Creator's name.

No unregarded star
　　Contracts its light
Into so small a character,
Remov'd far from our human sight :

But if we steadfast look
        We shall discern
In it, as in some holy book,
How man may heavenly knowledge learn.

It tells the conqueror,
        That far-stretched power,
Which his proud dangers traffic for,
Is but the triumph of an hour.

That from the farthest north,
        Some nation may
Yet undiscovered issue forth,
And o'er his new-got conquest sway.

Some nation yet shut in
        With hills of ice
May be let out to scourge his sin,
Till they shall equal him in vice.

And then they likewise shall
        Their ruin have ;
For as your selves your empires fall,
And every kingdom hath a grave.

Thus those celestial fires,
        Though seeming mute,

The fallacy of our desires
And all the pride of life confute.

For they have watched since first
The world had birth :
And found sin in itself accursed,
And nothing permanent on earth.

(113)

ROBERT HERRICK.

I DARE not ask a kiss;
  I dare not beg a smile;
Lest having that, or this,
  I might grow proud the while.

No, no, the utmost share
  Of my desire shall be
Only to kiss that air,
  That lately kissed thee.

(114)

GEORGE WITHER.

SHALL I, wasting in despair
Die, because a woman 's fair?
Or make pale my cheeks with care
'Cause another's rosy are?
    Be she fairer than the day
    Or the flowery meads in May,
    If she think not well of me,
    What care I how fair she be?

Shall my seely heart be pin'd
'Cause I see a woman kind?
Or a well-disposed nature
Joined with a lovely feature?
    Be she meeker, kinder than
    Turtle-dove or pelican:
    If she be not so to me,
    What care I how kind she be?

Shall a woman's virtues move
Me to perish for her love?
Or her well-deservings known
Make me quite forget mine own?
  Be she with that goodness blest
  Which may merit name of best:
  If she be not such to me,
  What care I how good she be?

'Cause her fortune seems too high
Shall I play the fool and die?
She that bears a noble mind,
If not outward helps she find,
  Thinks what with them he would do,
  That without them dares her woo.
  And unless that mind I see,
  What care I how great she be?

Great, or good, or kind, or fair
I will ne'er the more despair:
If she love me, this believe,
I will die ere she shall grieve.
  If she slight me when I woo,
  I can scorn and let her go,
  For if she be not for me,
  What care I for whom she be?

(115)

HENRY VAUGHAN.

I WALKED the other day to spend my hour,
    Into a field,
Where I sometimes had seen the soil to yield
    A gallant flower;
But winter now had ruffled all the bower
    And curious store
    I knew there heretofore.

Yet I, whose search loved not to peep and peer
    I' th' face of things,
Thought with myself, there might be other springs
    Besides this here,
Which, like cold friends, sees us but once a year;
    And so the flower
    Might have some other bower.

Then taking up what I could nearest spy
    I digged about
That place where I had seen him to grow out;

And by and by
I saw the warm recluse alone to lie,
        Where fresh and green
        He lived of us unseen.

Many a question intricate and rare
        Did I there strow;
But all I could extort was, that he now
        Did there repair
Such losses as befel him in this air,
        And would ere long
        Come forth most fair and young.

This past, I threw the clothes quite o'er his head;
        And stung with fear
Of my own frailty dropped down many a tear
        Upon his bed;
Then sighing whispered, *Happy are the dead!*
        What peace doth now
        Rock him asleep below!

And yet, how few believe such doctrine springs
        From a poor root,
Which all the winter sleeps here underfoot,
        And hath no wings
To raise it to the truth and light of things;
        But is still trod
        By every wandering clod.

O Thou ! whose Spirit did at first inflame
    And warm the dead,
And by a sacred incubation fed
    With life this frame,
Which once had neither being, form, nor name ;
    Grant I may so
    Thy steps track here below,

That in these masks and shadows I may see
    Thy sacred way ;
And by those hid ascents climb to that day,
    Which breaks from Thee
Who art in all things, though invisibly !
    Show me Thy peace,
    Thy mercy, love, and ease !

And from this care, where dreams and sorrows reign,
    Lead me above,
Where Light, Joy, Leisure, and true comforts move
    Without all pain ;
There, hid in Thee, show me his life again,
    At whose dumb urn
    Thus all the year I mourn.

(116)

WILLIAM HABINGTON

FINE young folly, though you were
That fair beauty I did swear,
    Yet you ne'er could reach my heart:
For we courtiers learn at school,
Only with your sex to fool;
    You are not worth the serious part.

When I sigh and kiss your hand,
Cross my arms, and wondering stand,
    Holding parley with your eye,
Then dilate on my desires,
Swear the sun ne'er shot such fires—
    All is but a handsome lie.

When I eye your curl or lace,
Gentle soul, you think your face
    Straight some murder doth commit;

And your virtue doth begin
To grow scrupulous of my sin,
    When I talk to show my wit.

Therefore, madam, wear no cloud,
Nor to check my love grow proud ;
    In sooth I much do doubt,
'Tis the powder in your hair,
Not your breath, perfumes the air,
    And your clothes that set you out.

Yet though truth has this confessed,
And I vow I love in jest,
    When I next begin to court,
And protest an amorous flame,
You will swear I in earnest am :
    Bedlam ! this is pretty sport.

(117)

ROBERT HERRICK.

COME, Anthea, let us two
Go to feast, as others do.
Tarts and custards, creams and cakes,
Are the junkets still at wakes :
Unto which the tribes resort,
Where the business is the sport :
Morris-dancers thou shalt see,
Marian too, in pageantry :
And a mimic to devise
Many grinning properties.
Players there will be, and those
Base in action as in clothes :
Yet with strutting they will please
The incurious villages.
Near the dying of the day,
There will be a cudgel-play,
Where a coxcomb will be broke,
Ere a good word can be spoke :
But the anger ends all here,
Drenched in ale, or drowned in beer.
Happy rustics, best content
With the cheapest merriment :
And possess no other fear,
Than to want the Wake next year.

(118)

Henry Vaughan.

They are all gone into the world of light !
    And I alone sit ling'ring here !
Their very memory is fair and bright,
    And my sad thoughts doth clear.

It glows and glitters in my cloudy breast
    Like stars upon some gloomy grove,
Or those faint beams in which this hill is drest
    After the Sun's remove.

I see them walking in an air of glory,
    Whose light doth trample on my days ;
My days, which are at best but dull and hoary,
    Mere glimmering and decays.

O holy Hope ! and high Humility !
    High as the Heavens above ;
These are your walks, and you have show'd them me
    To kindle my cold love.

Dear, beauteous death; the Jewel of the Just!
   Shining no where but in the dark;
What mysteries do lie beyond thy dust,
   Could man outlook that mark !

He that hath found some fledg'd bird's nest may know
   At first sight if the bird be flown;
But what fair dell or grove he sings in now,
   That is to him unknown.

And yet, as Angels in some brighter dreams
   Call to the soul when man doth sleep,
So some strange thoughts transcend our wonted
      themes,
   And into glory peep.

If a star were confin'd into a tomb,
   Her captive flames must needs burn there;
But when the hand that locked her up gives room,
   She 'll shine through all the sphere.

O Father of eternal life, and all
   Created glories under Thee !
Resume Thy spirit from this world of thrall
   Into true liberty !

Either disperse these mists, which blot and fill
   My perspective still as they pass;
Or else remove me hence unto that hill,
   Where I shall need no glass.

(119)

GEORGE HERBERT.

How sweetly doth 'My Master' sound! 'My Master!'
    As amber-grease leaves a rich scent
        Unto the taster,
    So do these words a sweet content,
An oriental fragrancy, 'My Master.'

With these all day I do perfume my mind,
    My mind even thrust into them both;
        That I might find
    What cordials make this curious broth,
This broth of smells, that feeds and fats my mind.

'My Master,' shall I speak? O that to Thee
    'My servant' were a little so,
        As flesh may be;
    That these two words might creep and grow
To some degree of spiciness to Thee!

Then should the pomander, which was before
    A speaking sweet, mend by reflection,
        And tell me more;

For pardon of my imperfection
Would warm and work it sweeter than before.

For when ‘ My Master,’ which alone is sweet,
    And ev’n in my unworthiness pleasing,
        Shall call and meet,
    ‘ My servant,’ as Thee not displeasing,
That call is but the breathing of the sweet.

This breathing would with gains, by sweetening me—
    As sweet things traffic when they meet—
        Return to Thee ;
    And so this new commerce and sweet
Should all my life employ and busy me.

(120)

JOHN FLETCHER.

ARM, arm, arm, arm ! the scouts are all come in ;
Keep your ranks close, and now your honours win.
Behold from yonder hill the foe appears ;
Bows, bills, glaves, arrows, shields, and spears !
Like a dark wood he comes, or tempest pouring ;
Oh, view the wings of horse the meadows scouring.
The vanguard marches bravely.   Hark, the drums !
                                        Dub, dub.
They meet, they meet, and now the battle comes :
                See how the arrows fly,
                That darken all the sky !
                Hark how the trumpets sound,
                Hark how the hills rebound,
                    Tara, tara, tara, tara, tara !

Hark how the horses charge ! in, boys, boys, in !
The battle totters ; now the wounds begin :
                Oh, how they cry !
                Oh, how they die !

Room for the valiant Memnon, armed with thunder !
    See how he breaks the ranks asunder !
They fly ! they fly !   Eumenes has the chase,
And brave Polybius makes good his place.
        To the plains, to the woods,
        To the rocks, to the floods,
They fly for succour.   Follow, follow, follow !
Hark how the soldiers hollow !   *Hey, hey !*
        Brave Diocles is dead,
        And all his soldiers fled ;
        The battle 's won, and lost,
        That many a life hath cost.

(121)

ANDREW MARVELL.

WHERE the remote Bermudas ride,
In the ocean's bosom unespied,
From a small boat, that rowed along,
The listening winds received this song.

'What should we do but sing His praise,
That led us through the watery maze,
Unto an isle so long unknown,
And yet far kinder than our own?
Where He the huge sea monsters wracks,
That lift the deeps upon their backs,
He lands us on a grassy stage,
Safe from the storms and prelates' rage.
He gave us this eternal spring
Which here enamels everything,
And sends the fowls to us in care,
On daily visits through the air;
He hangs in shades the orange bright,

O

Like golden lamps in a green night,
And does in the pomegranates close
Jewels more rich than Ormus shows;
He makes the figs our mouths to meet,
And throws the melons at our feet;
But apples plants of such a price,
No tree could ever bear them twice.
With cedars chosen by His hand
From Lebanon, He stores the land
And makes the hollow seas that roar
Proclaim the amber-grease on shore;
He cast (of which we rather boast)
The Gospel's pearl upon our coast,
And in these rocks for us did frame
A temple, where to sound His name.
Oh! let our voice His praise exalt,
Till it arrive at heaven's vault,
Which then, perhaps, rebounding may
Echo beyond the Mexique Bay.'

Thus sung they, in the English boat,
A holy and a cheerful note,
And all the way, to guide their chime,
With falling oars they kept the time.

(122)

ROBERT HERRICK.

Down with the rosemary and bays,
　　Down with the mistletoe;
Instead of holly, now up-raise
　　The greener box, for show.

The holly hitherto did sway;
　　Let box now domineer;
Until the dancing Easter-day,
　　Or Easter's Eve appear.

Then youthful box, which now hath grace,
　　Your houses to renew;
Grown old, surrender must his place,
　　Unto the crisped yew.

When yew is out, then birch comes in,
　　And many a flower beside;
Both of a fresh and fragrant kin
　　To honour Whitsuntide.

Green rushes then, and sweetest bents,
With cooler oaken boughs ;.
Come in for comely ornaments,
To re-adorn the house.
Thus times do shift ; each thing his turn does hold ;
New things succeed, as former things grow old.

(123)

HENRY VAUGHAN.

WITH what deep murmurs, through time's silent stealth,
Doth thy transparent, cool, and watery wealth
      Here flowing fall,
      And chide, and call,
As if his liquid, loose retinue stayed
Lingering, and were of this steep place afraid ;
      The common pass,
      Where, clear as glass,
      All must descend
      Not to an end,
But quickened by this deep and rocky grave,
Rise to a longer course more bright and brave.

    Dear stream ! dear bank ! where often I
    Have sat, and pleased my pensive eye ;
    Why, since each drop of thy quick store
    Runs thither whence it flowed before,
    Should poor souls fear a shade or night,
    Who came, sure, from a sea of light ?

Or, since those drops are all sent back
So sure to thee that none doth lack,
Why should frail flesh doubt any more
That what God takes He 'll not restore?

O useful element and clear!
My sacred wash and cleanser here;
My first consigner unto those
Fountains of life, where the Lamb goes!
What sublime truths and wholesome themes
Lodge in thy mystical, deep streams!
Such as dull man can never find,
Unless that Spirit lead his mind,
Which first upon thy face did move
And hatched all with His quickening love.
As this loud brook's incessant fall
In streaming rings restagnates all,
Which reach by course the bank, and then
Are no more seen : just so pass men.
O my invisible estate,
My glorious liberty, still late!
Thou art the channel my soul seeks,
Not this with cataracts and creeks.

(124)

PHINEAS FLETCHER.

LOVE is the sire, dam, nurse, and seed
Of all that earth, air, waters breed :
All these, earth, water, air, fire,
Though contraries, in love conspire.
Fond painters, love is not a lad
With bow, and shafts and feathers clad,
As he is fancied in the brain
Of some loose loving idle swain.
Much sooner is he felt than seen ;
His substance subtle, slight and thin.
Oft leaps he from the glancing eyes ;
Oft in some smooth mount he lies ;
Soonest he wins, the fastest flies ;
Oft lurks he 'twixt the ruddy lips,
Thence, while the heart his nectar sips,
Down to the soul the poison slips ;
Oft in a voice creeps down the ear ;
Oft hides his darts in golden hair ;

Oft blushing cheeks do light his fires ;
Oft in a smooth soft skin retires ;
Often in smiles, often in tears,
His flaming heat in water bears ;
When nothing else kindles desire,
Even virtue's self shall blow the fire.
Love with a thousand darts abounds,
Surest and deepest virtue wounds ;
Oft himself becomes a dart,
And love with love doth love impart.
Thou painful pleasure, pleasing pain,
Thou gainful loss, thou losing gain,
Thou bitter sweet, easing disease,
How dost thou by displeasing please ?
How dost thou thus bewitch the heart,
To love in hate, to joy in smart,
To think itself most bound when free,
And freest in its slavery ?
Every creature is thy debtor ;
None but loves, some worse, some better :
Only in love they happy prove
Who love what most deserves their love.

(125)

ROBERT HERRICK.

AH, Ben !
Say how, or when
　Shall we thy guests
Meet at those lyric feasts,
　Made at the Sun,
The Dog, the Triple Tun ?
Where we such clusters had,
As made us nobly wild, not mad ;
And yet each verse of thine
Out-did the meat, out-did the frolic wine.

My Ben !
Or come again :
　Or send to us,
Thy wits' great over-plus ;
　But teach us yet
Wisely to husband it ;
Lest we that talent spend :
And having once brought to an end
That precious stock ; the store
Of such a wit the world should have no more

(126)

GEORGE HERBERT.

THROW away Thy rod,
Throw away Thy wrath ;
  O my God,
Take the gentle path.

For my heart's desire
Unto Thine is bent ;
  I aspire
To a full consent.

Not a word or look
I affect to own,
    But by book
And Thy Book alone

Though I fail, I weep ;
Though I halt in pace
    Yet I creep
To the throne of grace

Then let wrath remove,
Love will do the deed ;
    For with love
Stony hearts will bleed.

Love is swift of foot ;
Love 's a man of war,
    And can shoot
And can hit from far.

Who can 'scape his bow ?
That which wrought on Thee,
    Brought Thee low,
Needs must work on me.

Throw away Thy rod :
Though man frailties hath,
    Thou art God,
Throw away Thy wrath.

(127)

THOMAS RANDOLPH.

COME, spur away,
I have no patience for a longer stay.
But must go down,
And leave the chargeable noise of this great town.
I will the country see,
Where old simplicity,
Though hid in gray,
Doth look more gay
Than foppery in plush and scarlet clad.
Farewell, you city wits, that are
Almost at civil war ;
'Tis time that I grow wise, when all the world grows
mad.

More of my days
I will not spend to gain an idiot's praise ;
Or to make sport
For some slight puisne of the Inns-of-Court.
Then, worthy Stafford, say,
How shall we spend the day ?

With what delights
Shorten the nights?
When from this tumult we are got secure,
Where mirth with all her freedom goes,
Yet shall no finger lose;
Where every word is thought, and every thought is
pure.

There from the tree
We 'll cherries pluck, and pick the strawberry.
And every day
Go see the wholesome country girls make hay,
Whose brown hath lovelier grace
Than any painted face,
That I do know
Hyde Park can show.
Where I had rather gain a kiss than meet
(Though some of them in greater state
Might court my love with plate)
The beauties of the Cheap, and wives of Lombard
Street.

But think upon
Some other pleasures : these to me are none.
Why do I prate
Of women, that are things against my fate?
I never mean to wed
That torture to my bed.

My muse is she
My love shall be.
Let clowns get wealth and heirs; when I am gone,
And the great bugbear, grisly death,
Shall take this idle breath,
If I a poem leave, that poem is my son.

Of this no more;
We 'll rather taste the bright Pomona's store.
No fruit shall 'scape
Our palates, from the damson to the grape.
Then, full, we 'll seek a shade,
And hear what music 's made;
How Philomel
Her tale doth tell,
And how the other birds do fill the quire:
The thrush and blackbird lend their throats
Warbling melodious notes;
We will all sports enjoy which others but desire.

Ours is the sky,
Whereat what fowl we please our hawk shall fly:
Nor will we spare
To hunt the crafty fox or timorous hare;
But let our hounds run loose
In any ground they 'll chóose,
The buck shall fall,
The stag, and all:

Our pleasures must from their own warrants be,
    For to my muse, if not to me,
    I'm sure all game is free :
Heaven, earth, are all but parts of her great royalty.

    And when we mean
To taste of Bacchus' blessings now and then,
    And drink by stealth
A cup or two to noble Barkley's health,
    I 'll take my pipe and try
    The Phrygian melody ;
    Which he that hears,
    Lets through his ears
A madness to distemper all the brain.
    Then I another pipe will take
    And Doric music make,
To civilise with graver notes our wits again.

(128)

ROBERT HERRICK.

IN the hour of my distress,
When temptations me oppress,
And when I my sins confess,
    Sweet Spirit, comfort me !

When I lie within my bed,
Sick in heart and sick in head,
And with doubts discomforted,
    Sweet Spirit, comfort me !

When the house doth sigh and weep,
And the world is drowned in sleep,
Yet mine eyes the watch do keep ;
    Sweet Spirit, comfort me !

When the artless doctor sees
Not one hope, but of his' fees,
And his skill runs on the lees ;
    Sweet Spirit, comfort me !

Robert Herrick

When his potion and his pill,
Has or none, or little skill,
Meet for nothing, but to kill ;
    Sweet Spirit, comfort me !

When the passing-bell doth toll,
And the furies in a shoal
Come to fright a parting soul ;
    Sweet Spirit, comfort me !

When the tapers now burn blue,
And the comforters are few,
And that number more than true ;
    Sweet Spirit, comfort me !

When the priest his last hath prayed,
And I nod to what is said,
'Cause my speech is now decayed ;
    Sweet Spirit, comfort me !

When (God knows) I'm tossed about,
Either with despair, or doubt ;
Yet before the glass be out,
    Sweet Spirit, comfort me !

When the Tempter me pursu'th
With the sins of all my youth,
And half damns me with untruth ;
    Sweet Spirit, comfort me !

When the flames and hellish cries
Fright mine ears and fright mine eyes,
And all terrors me surprise;
  Sweet Spirit, comfort me!

When the Judgment is revealed,
And that opened which was sealed,
When to Thee I have appealed;
  Sweet Spirit, comfort me!

(129)

GILES FLETCHER.

Love is the blossom where there blows
Every thing that lives or grows :
Love doth make the Heav'ns to move,
And the Sun doth burn in love :
Love the strong and weak doth yoke,
And makes the ivy climb the oak ;
Under whose shadows lions wild,
Soften'd by love, grow tame and mild :
Love no med'cine can appease,
He burns the fishes in the seas ;
Not all the skill his wounds can stench,
Not all the sea his fire can quench :
Love did make the bloody spear
Once a leavy coat to wear,
While in his leaves there shrouded lay
Sweet birds, for love that sing and play :
And of all love's joyful flame,
I the bud and blossom am.
    Only bend the knee to me,
    Thy wooing shall thy winning be.

See, see the flowers that below,
Now as fresh as morning blow,
And of all, the virgin rose,
That as bright Aurora shows:
How they all unleaved die,
Losing their virginity;
Like unto a summer-shade,
But now born, and now they fade.
Every thing doth pass away,
There is danger in delay:
Come, come gather then the rose,
Gather it, or it you lose.
All the sands of Tagus' shore
Into my bosom casts his ore:
All the valleys' swimming corn
To my house is yearly borne:
Every grape of every vine
Is gladly bruis'd to make me wine,
While ten thousand kings, as proud,
To carry up my train have bow'd,
And a world of ladies send me
In my chambers to attend me.
All the stars in Heav'n that shine,
And ten thousand more are mine:
    Only bend thy knee to me,
    Thy wooing shall thy winning be.

(130)

FRANCIS BEAUMONT.

MAY I find a woman fair,
And her mind as clear as air,
If her beauty go alone,
'Tis to me as if 't were none.

May I find a woman rich,
And not of too high a pitch :
If that pride should cause disdain,
Tell me, lover, where 's thy gain ?

May I find a woman wise,
And her falsehood not disguise ;
Hath she Wit as well as Will,
Double arm'd she is to ill.

May I find a woman kind,
And not wavering like the wind :
How should I call that love mine,
When 'tis his, and his, and thine ?

May I find a woman true,
There is beauty's fairest hue ;
There is beauty, love, and wit,
Happy he can compass it.

(131)

ROBERT HERRICK.

IN this world, the Isle of Dreams,
While we sit by sorrow's streams,
Tears and terrors are our themes
              Reciting :

But when once from hence we fly,
More and more approaching nigh
Unto young Eternity
              Uniting :

In that whiter Island, where
Things are evermore sincere ;
Candour here, and lustre there
              Delighting :

There no monstrous fancies shall
Out of hell an horror call,
To create, or cause at all
              Affrighting.

There in calm and cooling sleep
We our eyes shall never steep;
But eternal watch shall keep,
               Attending.

Pleasures, such as shall pursue
Me immortalised, and you;
And fresh joys, as never too
               Have ending.

(132)

FRANCIS BEAUMONT.

NEVER more will I protest
To love a woman but in jest:
For as they cannot be true,
So to give each man his due,
    When the wooing fit is past,
    Their affection cannot last.

Therefore if I chance to meet
With a mistress fair and sweet,
She my service shall obtain,
Loving her for love again :
    This much liberty I crave
    Not to be a constant slave.

But when we have tried each other,
If she better like another,
Let her quickly change for me,
Then to change am I as free.
    He or she that loves too long
    Sell their freedom for a song.

(133)

HENRY KING.

TELL me no more how fair she is,
　I have no mind to hear
The story of that distant bliss
　I never shall come near :
By sad experience I have found
That her perfection is my wound.

And tell me not how fond I am
　To tempt my daring fate,
From whence no triumph ever came,
　But to repent too late :
There is some hope ere long I may
In silence dote myself away.

I ask no pity, Love, from thee,
　Nor will thy justice blame,
So that thou wilt not envy me
　The glory of my flame :
Which crowns my heart whene'er it dies,
In that it falls her sacrifice.

(·134)

ROBERT HERRICK.

THANKSGIVING for a former, doth invite
God to bestow a second benefit.

(135)

ABRAHAM COWLEY.

MARGARITA first possessed,
    If I remember well, my breast,
    Margarita first of all ;
But when awhile the wanton maid
With my restless heart had played,
    Martha took the flying ball.

Martha soon did it resign
    To the beauteous Catharine.
    Beauteous Catharine gave place
(Though loth and angry she to part
With the possession of my heart)
    To Elisa's conquering face.

Elisa till this hour might reign
    Had she not evil counsels ta'en.
    Fundamental laws she broke,
And still new favourites she chose,
Till up in arms my passions rose,
    And cast away her yoke.

Mary then and gentle Anne
    Both to reign at once began.
    Alternately they swayed,
And sometimes Mary was the fair,
And sometimes Anne the crown did wear,
    And sometimes both I obeyed.

Another Mary then arose
    And did rigorous laws impose.
    A mighty tyrant she!
Long, alas, should I have been,
Under that iron-sceptred Queen,
    Had not Rebecca set me free.

When fair Rebecca set me free,
    'Twas then a golden time with me
    But soon those pleasures fled,
For the gracious Princess died
In her youth and beauty's pride,
    And Judith reigned in her stead.

One month, three days, and half an hour
    Judith held the sovereign power.
    Wondrous beautiful her face,
But so small and weak her wit,
That she to govern was unfit,
    And so Susanna took her place.

But when Isabella came
    Armed with a resistless flame
    And th' artillery of her eye ;
Whilst she proudly marched about
Greater conquests to find out,
    She beat out Susan by the by.

But in her place I then obeyed
    Black-eyed Bess, her viceroy-maid,
    To whom ensued a vacancy,
Thousand worse passions then possessed
The interregnum of my breast.
    Bless me from such an anarchy !

Gentle Henrietta then
    And a third Mary next began,
    Then Joan, and Jane, and Audria.
And then a pretty Thomasine,
And then another Catharine,
    And then a long et cætera.

But should I now to you relate,
    The strength and riches of their state,
    The powder, patches, and the pins,
The ribbons, jewels, and the rings,
The lace, the paint, and warlike things
    That make up all their magazines ;

If I should tell the politic arts
    To take and keep men's hearts,
    The letters, embassies, and spies,
The frowns, and smiles, and flatteries,
The quarrels, tears, and perjuries,
    Numberless, nameless mysteries!

And all the little lime twigs laid
    By Matchavil, the waiting-maid;
    I more voluminous should grow
(Chiefly if I like them should tell
All change of weathers that befel)
    Than Holinshed, or Stow.

But I will briefer with them be,
    Since few of them were long with me.
    An higher and a nobler strain
My present Emperess dost claim,
Heleonora, first o' the name;
    Whom God grant long to reign!

(136)

EDMUND WALLER

Go, lovely Rose,
Tell her that wastes her time and me,
That now she knows
When I resemble her to thee
How sweet and fair she seems to be.

Tell her that's young,
And shuns to have her graces spied,
That hadst thou sprung
In deserts where no men abide,
Thou must have uncommended died.

Small is the worth
Of beauty from the light retired;
Bid her come forth,
Suffer herself to be desired,
And not so blush to be admired.

Then die, that she
The common fate of all things rare
May read in thee,
How small a part of time they share
Who are so wondrous sweet and fair.

(137)

Alexander Brome

Tell me not of a face that 's fair,
  Nor lip and cheek that 's red,
Nor of the tresses of her hair,
  Nor curls in order laid ;
Nor of a rare seraphic voice,
  That like an angel sings ;
Though if I were to take my choice,
  I would have all these things.
But if that thou wilt have me love,
  And it must be a she :
The only argument can move
  Is, that she will love me.

The glories of your ladies be
  But metaphors of things,
And but resemble what we see
  Each common object brings.
Roses out-red their lips and cheeks,
  Lilies their whiteness stain :
What fool is he that shadow seeks,
  And may the substance gain !
Then if thou 'lt have me love a lass,
  Let it be one that 's kind,
Else I'm a servant to the glass,
  That 's with Canary lin'd.

(138)

ABRAHAM COWLEY.

I NEVER yet could see that face
   Which had no dart for me;
From fifteen years, to fifty's space,
   They all victorious be.
Love! thou 'rt a devil, if I may call thee one;
For sure in me thy name is Legion.

Colour, or shape, good limbs, or face,
   Goodness, or wit, in all I find;
In motion, or in speech, a grace;
   If all fail, yet 'tis woman-kind;
And I 'm so weak, the pistol need not be
Double or treble charg'd to murder me.

If tall, the name of Proper slays,
   If fair, she 's pleasant in the light;
If low, her prettiness does please,
   If black, what lover loves not night?
If yellow-haired, I love, lest it should be
Th' excuse to others for not loving me.

Q

The fat, like plenty, fills my heart;
    The lean, with love makes me too so:
If straight, her body 's Cupid's dart
    To me; if crooked, 'tis his bow:
Nay, age itself does me to rage incline,
And strength to women gives, as well as wine.

Just half as large as Charity
    My richly landed Love 's become;
And, judg'd aright, is Constancy,
    Though it take up a larger room:
Him, who loves always one, why should they call
More constant than the man loves always all?

Thus with unwearied wings I flee
    Through all Love's gardens and his fields;
And, like the wise, industrious bee,
    No weed but honey to me yields!
Honey still spent this diligence still supplies,
Though I return not home with laden thighs.

My soul at first indeed did prove
    Of pretty strength against a dart,
Till I this habit got of love;
    But my consum'd and wasted heart,
Once burnt to tinder with a strong desire,
Since that, by every spark is set on fire.

(139)

WILLIAM BROWNE.

VENUS by Adonis' side
Crying kist and kissing cried,
Wrung her hands and tore her hair
For Adonis dying there.

'Stay,' quoth she, 'O stay and live !
Nature surely doth not give
To the earth her sweetest flowers
To be seen but some few hours.'

On his face, still as he bled
For each drop a tear she shed,
Which she kist or wip'd away,
Else had drown'd him where he lay.

'Fair Proserpina,' quoth she,
'Shall not have thee yet from me ;
Nor thy soul to fly begin
While my lips can keep it in.'

Here she clos'd again.   And some
Say, Apollo would have come
To have cur'd his wounded limb,
But that she had smother'd him.

(140)

THOMAS CAREW.

I WAS foretold, your rebel sex
  Nor love nor pity knew,
And with what scorn you use to vex
  Poor hearts that humbly sue ;
Yet I believ'd to crown our pain,
  Could we the fortress win,
The happy lover sure would gain
  A paradise within.
I thought love's plagues like dragons sate,
Only to fright us at the gate.

But I did enter, and enjoy
  What happy lovers prove,
For I could kiss, and sport, and toy,
  And taste those sweets of love,
Which, had they but a lasting state,
  Or if in Celia's breast
The force of love might not abate,

Jove were too mean a guest.
But now her breach of faith far more
Afflicts, than did her scorn before.

Hard fate ! to have been once possest,
   As victor, of a heart
Achiev'd with labour and unrest,
   And then forc'd to depart !
If the stout foe will not resign
   When I besiege a town,
I lose but what was never mine.
   But he that is cast down
From enjoy'd beauty, feels a woe
Only deposèd kings can know.

(141)

RICHARD CORBET.

FAREWELL rewards and fairies,
  Good housewives now may say,
For now foul sluts in dairies
  Do fare as well as they.
And though they sweep their hearths no less
  Than maids were wont to do,
Yet who of late for cleanliness,
  Finds sixpence in her shoe?

Lament, lament, old abbeys,
  The fairies lost command;
They did but change priests' babies,
  But some have chang'd your land;
And all your children sprung from thence
  Are now grown Puritans,
Who live as changelings ever since
  For love of your domains.

At morning and at evening both
  You merry were and glad,

So little care of sleep or sloth
 These pretty ladies had ;
When Tom came home from labour,
 Or Ciss to milking rose,
Then merrily merrily went their tabor,
 And nimbly went their toes.

Witness those rings and roundelays
 Of theirs, which yet remain,
Were footed in Queen Mary's days
 On many a grassy plain ;
But since of late, Elizabeth,
 And later, James came in,
They never danc'd on any heath
 As when the time hath bin.

By which we note the fairies
 Were of the old profession ;
Their songs were Ave Marys ;
 Their dances were procession :
But now, alas ! they all are dead
 Or gone beyond the seas ;
Or farther for religion fled,
 Or else they take their ease.

A tell-tale in their company
 They never could endure,

And whoso kept not secretly
   Their mirth, was punish'd sure;
It was a just and Christian deed
   To pinch such black and blue:
O how the commonwealth doth need
   Such justices as you!

Now they have left our quarters
   A register they have,
Who looketh to their charters,
   A man both wise and grave;
A hundred of their merry pranks
   By one that I could name
Are kept in store, con twenty thanks
   To William for the same.

I marvel who his cloak would turn
   When Puck had led him round,
Or where those walking fires would burn,
   Where Cureton would be found;
How Broker would appear to be,
   For whom this age doth mourn;
But that their spirits live in thee,
   In thee, old William Chourne.

To William Chourne of Staffordshire
   Give laud and praises due,

Who every meal can mend your cheer
  With tales both old and true :
To William all give audience,
  And pray ye for his noddle,
For all the fairies' evidence
  Were lost, if that were addle.

(142)

William Drummond.

Phœbus, arise,
And paint the sable skies
With azure, white, and red ;
Rouse Memnon's mother from her Tithon's bed,
That she thy career may with roses spread ;
The nightingales thy coming eachwhere sing ;
Make an eternal spring,
Give life to this dark world which lieth dead ;
Spread forth thy golden hair
In larger locks than thou wast wont before,
And, emperor-like, decore
With diadem of pearl thy temples fair :
Chase hence the ugly night,
Which serves but to make dear thy glorious light.
This is that happy morn
That day, long-wishèd day,
Of all my life so dark
(If cruel stars have not my ruin sworn,
And fates not hope betray),

Which, only white, deserves
A diamond for ever should it mark :
This is the morn should bring unto this grove
My love, to hear and recompense my love.
Fair king, who all preserves,
But show thy blushing beams,
And thou two sweeter eyes
Shalt see, than those which by Peneus' streams
Did once thy heart surprise ;
Nay, suns, which shine as clear
As thou when twice thou did to Rome appear.
Now, Flora, deck thyself in fairest guise ;
If that ye, winds, would hear
A voice surpassing fair Amphion's lyre,
Your stormy chiding stay ;
Let zephyr only breathe,
And with her tresses play,
Kissing sometimes these purple ports of death.
The winds all silent are,
And Phœbus in his chair,
Ensaffroning sea and air,
Makes vanish every star :
Night like a drunkard reels
Beyond the hills to shun his flaming wheels ;
The fields with flowers are decked in every hue,
The clouds bespangle with bright gold their blue :
Here is the pleasant place,
And every thing, save her, who all should grace

(143)

ALEXANDER BROME.

'TIS true, I never was in love :
    But now I mean to be,
        For there 's no art
        Can shield a heart
    From love's supremacy.

Though in my nonage I have seen
    A world of taking faces,
I had not age or wit to ken
    Their several hidden graces.

Those virtues which, though thinly set,
    In others are admired,
In thee are altogether met,
    Which make thee so desired.

That though I never was in love,
    Nor never meant to be,
        Thyself and parts
        Above my arts
    Have drawn my heart to thee.

(144)

RICHARD CRASHAW.

WHAT bright soft thing is this?
Sweet Mary, thy fair eyes' expense?
  A moist spark it is,
A wat'ry diamond; from whence
The very term, I think, was found
The water of a diamond.

O 'tis not a tear,
'Tis a star about to drop
  From thine eyes its sphere;
The Sun will stoop and take it up.
Proud will his sister be to wear
This thine eye's jewel in her ear.

O 'tis a tear,
Too true a tear; for no sad eyne,
  How sad soe'er,
Rain so true a tear as thine;
Each drop leaving a place so dear,
Weeps for itself, is its own tear.

Such a pearl as this is,
(Slipt from Aurora's dewy breast)
    The rosebud's sweet lip kisses ;
And such the rose itself, when vext
With ungentle flames, does shed,
Sweating in too warm a bed.

Such the maiden gem
By the wanton spring put on,
    Peeps from her parent stem,
And blushes on the wat'ry sun :
This wat'ry blossom of thine eyne,
Ripe, will make the richer wine.

Fair drop, why quak'st thou so ?
'Cause thou straight must lay thy head
    In the dust ? Oh no :
The dust shall never be thy bed :
A pillow for thee will I bring,
Stuff'd with down of angel's wing.

Thus carried up on high
(For to Heaven thou must go)
    Sweetly shalt thou lie,
And in soft slumbers bathe thy woe ;
Till the singing orbs awake thee,
And one of their bright chorus make thee.

There thyself shalt be
An eye, but not a weeping one,
Yet I doubt of thee,
Whether th' hadst rather there have shone
An eye of Heaven ; or still shine here
In the heav'n of Mary's eye, a tear.

(145)

William Drummond.

To the delightful green
Of you, fair radiant e'en,
Let each black yield beneath the starry arch.
Eyes, burnished Heavens of love,
Sinople lamps of Jove,
Save all those hearts which with your flames you
parch
Two burning suns you prove;
All other eyes, compared to you, dear lights,
Are Hells, or if not Hells, yet dumpish nights.
The Heavens (if we their glass
The sea believe) are green, not perfect blue;
They make all fair whatever fair there was,
And they are fair because they look like you.

(146)

ROBERT HERRICK.

Ye have been fresh and green,
  Ye have been fill'd with flowers;
And ye the walks have been
  Where maids have spent their hours.

You have beheld how they
  With wicker arks did come
To kiss and bear away
  The richer cowslips home.

Ye 've heard them sweetly sing,
  And seen them in a round;
Each virgin, like a spring,
  With honeysuckles crowned.

But now, we see none here,
  Whose silv'ry feet did tread,
And with dishevelled hair
  Adorned this smoother mead

R

Like unthrifts, having spent
  Your stock, and needy grown,
Ye 're left here to lament
  Your poor estates, alone.

(147)

RICHARD CRASHAW.

WHOE'ER she be,
That not impossible she,
That shall command my heart and me;

Where'er she lie,
Lock'd up from mortal eye,
In shady leaves of destiny:

Till that ripe birth
Of studied Fate stand forth,
And teach her fair steps to our Earth;

Till that divine
Idea take a shrine
Of crystal flesh, through which to shine:

Meet you her, my wishes,
Bespeak her to my blisses,
And be ye call'd, my absent kisses.

I wish her beauty,
That owes not all its duty
To gaudy tire, or glist'ring shoe-tie.

Something more than
Taffata or tissue can,
Or rampant feather, or rich fan.

More than the spoil
Of shop, or silkworm's toil,
Or a bought blush, or a set smile.

A face that 's best
By its own beauty drest,
And can alone command the rest.

A face made up
Out of no other shop,
Than what Nature's white hand sets ope.

A cheek where youth,
And blood, with pen of truth,
Write, what the reader sweetly ru'th.

A cheek where grows
More than a morning rose :
Which to no box his being owes.

Lips, where all day
A lover's kiss may play,
Yet carry nothing thence away.

Looks that oppress
Their richest tires, but dress
And clothe their simple nakedness.

Eyes, that displaces
The neighbour diamond, and out-faces
That sunshine by their own sweet graces.

Tresses, that wear
Jewels, but to declare
How much themselves more precious are.

Whose native ray
Can tame the wanton day
Of gems, that in their bright shades play.

Each ruby there,
Or pearl that dare appear,
Be its own blush, be its own tear.

A well-tam'd heart,
For whose more noble smart
Love may be long choosing a dart.

Eyes, that bestow
Full quivers on Love's bow ,
Yet pay less arrows than they owe.

Smiles, that can warm
The blood, yet teach a charm,
That chastity shall take no harm.

Blushes, that bin
The burnish of no sin,
Nor flames of aught too hot within.

Joys, that confess
Virtue their mistress,
And have no other head to dress.

Fears, fond and flight,
As the coy bride's, when night
First does the longing lover right.

Tears, quickly fled,
And vain, as those are shed
For a dying maidenhead.

Days, that need borrow
No part of their good morrow,
From a fore-spent night of sorrow.

Days, that in spite
Of darkness, by the light
Of a clear mind are day all night.

Nights, sweet as they,
Made short by lovers' play,
Yet long by th' absence of the day.

Life, that dares send
A challenge to his end,
And when it comes, say, ' Welcome, friend.'

Sydneian showers
Of sweet discourse, whose powers
Can crown old Winter's head with flowers.

Soft silken hours,
Open suns, shady bow'rs,
'Bove all, nothing within that low'rs.

Whate'er delight
Can make day's forehead bright,
Or give down to the wings of night.

In her whole frame
Have Nature all the name,
Art and ornament all the shame.

Her flattery,
Picture and poesy:
Her counsel her own virtue be.

I wish her store
Of worth may leave her poor
Of wishes; and I wish—no more.

Now if Time knows
That her whose radiant brows
Weave them a garland of my vows;

Her whose just bays
My future hopes can raise,
A trophy to her present praise;

Her that dares be
What these lines wish to see:
I seek no further, it is she.

'Tis she, and here,
Lo! I unclothe and clear
My wishes' cloudy character.

May she enjoy it,
Whose merit dare apply it,
But modesty dares still deny it.

Richard Crashaw

Such worth as this is,
Shall fix my flying wishes,
And determine them to kisses.

Let her full glory,
My fancies, fly before ye,
Be ye my fictions ; but her story.

(148)

WILLIAM BROWNE.

STEER hither, steer your wingèd pines
All beaten mariners,
Here lie love's undiscovered mines
A prey to passengers.
Perfumes far sweeter than the best
Which make the Phœnix' urn and nest :
Fear not your ships,
Nor any to oppose you save our lips.
But come on shore
Where no joy dies till love hath gotten more.

For swelling waves our panting breasts,
Where never storms arise,
Exchange and be awhile our guests :
For stars gaze on our eyes.
The compass love shall hourly sing,
And as he goes about the ring
We will not miss
To tell each point he nameth with a kiss.
Then come on shore,
Where no joy dies till love hath gotten more.

(149)

SIR EDWARD SHERBURNE.

Thou gav'st me late to eat
A sweet without but within bitter meat,
As if thou would'st have said ' Here, taste in this
What Celia is.'

But if there ought to be
A likeness (dearest) 'twixt thy gift and thee,
Why first the sweet in thee should I not taste—
The bitter last ?

(150)

SIR CHARLES SEDLEY.

AH, Chloris ! that I now could sit
  As unconcerned, as when
Your infant beauty could beget
  No pleasure nor no pain.

When I the dawn used to admire,
  And praised the coming day,
I little thought the growing fire
  Must take my rest away.

Your charms in harmless childhood lay,
  Like metals in the mine :
Age from no face took more away,
  Than youth concealed in thine.

But as your charms insensibly
  To their perfection pressed,
Fond love as unperceived did fly,
  And in my bosom rest.

My passion with your beauty grew,
　And Cupid at my heart,
Still, as his mother favoured you,
　Threw a new flaming dart.

Each gloried in their wanton part :
　To make a lover, he
Employed the utmost of his art—
　To make a beauty, she.

Though now I slowly bend to love,
　Uncertain of my fate,
If your fair self my chains approve,
　I shall my freedom hate.

Lovers, like dying men, may well
　At first disordered be ;
Since none alive can truly tell
　What fortune they must see.

(151)

SIR WILLIAM KILLIGREW.

COME, come, thou glorious object of my sight,
Oh my joy! my life, my only delight!
  May this glad minute be
  Blessed to eternity.
See how the glimmering tapers of the sky,
Do gaze, and wonder at our constancy,
  How they crowd to behold
  What our arms do unfold!

How do all envy our felicities!
And grudge the triumphs of Selindra's eyes:
  How Cynthia seeks to shroud
  Her crescent in yon cloud!

Where sad night puts her sable mantle on,
Thy light mistaking, hasteth to be gone;
  Her gloomy shades give way,
  As at the approach of day;

And all the planets shrink, in doubt to be
Eclipsèd by a brighter deity.

> Look, oh look !
>> How the small
>> Lights do fall,
>> And adore,
>> What before
> The heavens have not shown,
> Nor their godheads known !

> Such a faith,
>> Such a love
>> As may move
>> From above
> To descend ; and remain
> Amongst mortals again.

(152)

JOHN DRYDEN.

You charmed me not with that fair face,
    Though it was all divine :
To be another's is the grace
    That makes me wish you mine.
The gods and fortune take their part,
    Who, like young monarchs, fight,
And boldly dare invade that heart,
    Which is another's right.
First, mad with hope, we undertake
    To pull up every bar ;
But, once possessed, we faintly make
    A dull defensive war.
Now, every friend is turned a foe,
    In hope to get our store :
And passion makes us coward grow,
    Which made us brave before.

(153)

SIR CHARLES SEDLEY.

'HEARS not my Phillis how the birds
    Their feathered mates salute?
They tell their passion in their words,
    Must I alone be mute?'
        Phillis, without frown or smile,
        Sat and knotted all the while.

'The god of Love in thy bright eyes
    Does like a tyrant reign,
But in thy heart a child he lies
    Without his dart or flame.'
        Phillis, without frown or smile,
        Sat and knotted all the while.

'So many months in silence past,
    And yet in raging love,
Might well deserve one word at last
    My passion should approve.'

Phillis, without frown or smile,
Sat and knotted all the while.

'Must then your faithful swain expire
And not one look obtain,
Which he to soothe his fond desire
Might pleasingly explain?'
Phillis, without frown or smile,
Sat and knotted all the while!

(154)

CHARLES COTTON.

JOIN once again, my Celia, join
Thy rosy lips to these of mine,
  Which, though they be not such,
Are full as sensible of bliss,
That is, as soon can taste a kiss,
  As thine of softer touch.

Each kiss of thine creates desire,
Thy odorous breath inflames love's fire,
  And wakes the sleeping coal :
Such a kiss to be I find
The conversation of the mind,
  And whisper of the soul.

Thanks, sweetest, now thou 'rt perfect grown,
For by this last kiss I 'm undone ;
  Thou breathest silent darts,
Henceforth each little touch will prove
A dangerous stratagem in love,
  And thou wilt blow up hearts.

(155)

APHRA BEHN.

LOVE in fantastic triumph sat,
　　Whilst bleeding hearts around him flowed,
For whom fresh pains he did create,
　　And strange tyrannic power he showed;
From thy bright eyes he took his fires,
　　Which round about in sport he hurled;
But 'twas from mine he took desires
　　Enough to undo the amorous world.

From me he took his sighs and tears,
　　From thee his pride and cruelty,
From me his languishment and fears,
　　And every killing dart from thee;
Thus thou and I the god have armed,
　　And set him up a deity,
But my poor heart alone is harmed,
　　While thine the victor is, and free.

(156)

JOHN DRYDEN.

DAMON.

CELIMENA, of my heart
None shall e'er bereave you :
If, with your good leave, I may
Quarrel with you once a day,
I will never leave you.

, CELIMENA.

Passion's but an empty name,
Where respect is wanting :
Damon, you mistake your aim ;
Hang your heart, and burn your flame,
If you must be ranting.

DAMON.

Love as dull and muddy is,
As decaying liquor :

Anger sets it on the lees,
And refines it by degrees,
Till it works the quicker.

CELIMENA.

Love by quarrels to beget
Wisely you endeavour,
With a grave physician's wit,
Who, to cure an ague fit,
Put me in a fever.

DAMON.

Anger rouses love to fight,
And his only bait is,
'Tis the spur to dull delight,
And is but an eager bite,
When desire at height is.

CELIMENA

If such drops of heat can fall
In our wooing weather;
If such drops of heat can fall,
We shall have the devil and all
When we come together.

(157)

CHARLES COTTON.

CELIA, my fairest Celia, fell,
   Celia, than the fairest, fairer;
   Celia, with none I must compare her
   That all alone is all in all,
   Of what we fair and modest call;
   Celia, white as alabaster,
   Celia, than Diana chaster;
This fair, fair Celia, grief to tell,
This fair, this modest, chaste one, fell.

My Celia, sweetest Celia, fell
   As I have seen a snow-white dove
   Decline her bosom from above,
   And down her spotless body fling
   Without the motion of the wing,
   Till she arrest her seeming fall
   Upon some happy pedestal:
So soft, this sweet I love so well,
This sweet, this dove-like Celia, fell.

Celia, my dearest Celia, fell,
  As I have seen a melting star
  Drop down its fire from its sphere,
  Rescuing so its glorious sight
  From that paler snuff of light :
  Yet is a star bright and entire,
  As when 'twas wrapt in all that fire :
So bright, this dear I love so well,
This dear, this star-like Celia, fell.

And yet my Celia did not fall
  As grosser earthly mortals do,
  But stoop'd, like Phœbus, to renew
  Her lustre by her morning rise,
  And dart new beauties in the skies.
  Like a white dove, she took her flight,
  And, like a star, she shot her light :
This dove, this star, so lov'd of all,
My fair, dear, sweetest, did not fall.

But, if you 'll say my Celia fell,
  Of this I'm sure, that, like the dart
  Of Love it was, and on my heart ;
  Poor heart, alas ! wounded before,
  She needed not have hurt it more :
  So absolute a conquest she
  Had gain'd before of it, and me,
That neither of us have been well
Before, or since my Celia fell.

(158)

EARL OF ROCHESTER.

I CANNOT change, as others do,
    Though you unjustly scorn,
Since that poor swain that sighs for you,
    For you alone was born ;
No, Phillis, no, your heart to move
    A surer way I 'll try,—
And to revenge my slighted love,
    Will still love on, and die.

When, killed with grief, Amintas lies,
    And you to mind shall call
The sighs that now unpitied rise,
    The tears that vainly fall :
That welcome hour that ends his smart,
    Will then begin your pain,
For such a faithful tender heart
    Can never break in vain.

(159)

Earl of Dorset.

Phillis, for shame, let us improve
  A thousand different ways
Those few short moments snatched by love
  From many tedious days.

If you want courage to despise
  The censure of the grave,
Though love's a tyrant in your eyes
  Your heart is but a slave.

My love is full of noble pride,
  Nor can it e'er submit
To let that fop, Discretion, ride
  In triumph over it.

False friends I have, as well as you,
  Who daily counsel me

Fame and ambition to pursue,
   And leave off loving thee.

But when the least regard I show
   To fools who thus advise,
May I be dull enough to grow
   Most miserably wise.

(160)

John Dryden.

Calm was the even, and clear was the sky,
    And the new budding flowers did spring,
When all alone went Amyntas and I,
    To hear the sweet nightingale sing :
I sate, and he laid him down by me,
    But scarcely his breath could he draw ;
For when with a fear, he began to draw near,
    He was dashed with, Aha, ha, ha, ha !

He blushed to himself, and lay still for awhile,
    And his modesty curbed his desire ;
But straight I convinced all his fear with a smile,
    Which added new flames to his fire.
'O Sylvia,' said he, 'you are cruel,
    To keep your poor lover in awe ! '
Then once more he prest with his hand to my breast,
    But was dashed with, Aha, ha, ha, ha !

I knew 'twas his passion that caused all his fear,
  And therefore I pitied his case;
I whispered him softly, 'There's nobody near,'
  And laid my cheek close to his face:
But as he grew bolder and bolder,
  A shepherd came by us and saw;
And just as our bliss we began with a kiss,
  He laughed out with, Aha, ha, ha, ha!

(161)

EARL OF DORSET.

To all you ladies now at land
   We men at sea indite;
But first would have you understand
   How hard it is to write;
The Muses now, and Neptune too,
We must implore to write to you.

For though the Muses should prove kind,
   And fill our empty brain,
Yet if rough Neptune rouse the wind
   To wave the azure main,
Our paper, pen, and ink, and we,
Roll up and down our ships at sea.

Then if we write not by each post,
   Think not we are unkind,
Nor yet conclude our ships are lost
   By Dutchmen, or by wind;
Our tears we'll send a speedier way,
The tide shall waft them twice a day.

The King with wonder and surprise
   Will swear the seas grow bold,
Because the tides will higher rise,
   Than e'er they did of old ;
But let him know it is our tears
Bring floods of grief to Whitehall-stairs.

Should foggy Opdam chance to know
   Our sad and dismal story,
The Dutch would scorn so weak a foe,
   And quit their fort at Goree,
For what resistance can they find
From men who 've left their hearts behind ?

Let wind and weather do its worst,
   Be you to us but kind,
Let Dutchmen vapour, Spaniards curse,
   No sorrow we shall find ;
'Tis then no matter how things go,
Or who 's our friend, or who 's our foe.

To pass our tedious hours away,
   We throw a merry main,
Or else at serious ombre play,
   But why should we in vain
Each other's ruin thus pursue ?
We were undone when we left you !

But now our fears tempestuous grow
　　And cast our hopes away,
Whilst you, regardless of our woe,
　　Sit careless at a play,—
Perhaps permit some happier man
To kiss your hand or flirt your fan.

When any mournful tune you hear,
　　That dies in every note,
As if it sighed with each man's care,
　　For being so remote,
Think then how often love we 've made
To you, when all those tunes were played.

In justice you can not refuse
　　To think of our distress,
When we for hopes of honour lose
　　Our certain happiness ;
All those designs are but to prove
Ourselves more worthy of your love.

And now we 've told you all our loves,
　　And likewise all our fears,
In hopes this declaration moves
　　Some pity from your tears :
Let 's hear of no inconstancy,
We have too much of that at sea.

(162)

SIR WILLIAM DAVENANT.

'TIS, in good sooth, a most wonderful thing
  (I am even ashamed to relate it)
That love so many vexations should bring,
  And yet few have the wit to hate it.

Love's weather in maids should seldom hold fair :
  Like April's mine shall quickly alter ;
I 'll give him to-night a lock of my hair,
  To whom next day I 'll send a halter.

I cannot abide these malapert males,
  Pirates of love who know no duty ;
Yet love with a storm can take down their sails,
  And they must strike to Admiral Beauty.

Farewell to that maid who will be undone,
  Who in markets of men (where plenty
Is cried up and down) will die even for one ;
  I will live to make fools of twenty.

T

(163)

JOHN DRYDEN.

HEAR, ye sullen powers below :
  Hear, ye taskers of the dead.
You that boiling cauldrons blow,
  You that scum the molten lead.
You that pinch with red-hot tongs ;
You that drive the trembling hosts
  Of poor, poor ghosts,
With your sharpened prongs ;
You that thrust them off the brim ;
You that plunge them when they swim :
Till they drown ;
  Till they go
  On a row,
  Down, down, down :
Ten thousand, thousand, thousand fathoms low.
  Chorus—Till they drown, etc.

Music for awhile
Shall your cares beguile :
Wondering how your pains were eased ;
And disdaining to be pleased ;
Till Alecto free the dead
    From their eternal bands ;
Till the snakes drop from her head,
    And whip from out her hands.
Come away,
    Do not stay,
    But obey,
    While we play,
For hell 's broke up, and ghosts have holiday.
    Chorus—Come away, etc.

(164)

EARL OF DORSET.

DORINDA'S sparkling wit and eyes
    United cast too fierce a light,
Which blazes high, but quickly dies,
    Pains not the heart, but hurts the sight.

Love is a calmer, gentler joy,
    Smooth are his looks, and soft his pace,
Her Cupid is a blackguard boy,
    That runs his link full in your face.

(165)

JOHN DRYDEN.

FAREWELL, ungrateful traitor !
  Farewell, my perjured swain !
Let never injured creature
  Believe a man again.
The pleasure of possessing
Surpasses all expressing,
But 'tis too short a blessing,
  And love too long a pain.

'Tis easy to deceive us,
  In pity of your pain ;
But when we love, you leave us,
  To rail at you in vain.
Before we have descried it,
There is no bliss beside it,
But she, that once has tried it,
  Will never love again.

The passion you pretended,
    Was only to obtain ;
But when the charm is ended,
    The charmer you disdain.
Your love by ours we measure,
Till we have lost our treasure ;
But dying is a pleasure,
    When living is a pain.

(166)

SIR CHARLES SEDLEY.

Love still has something of the sea,
　From whence his mother rose ;
No time his slaves from love can free,
　Nor give their thoughts repose.

They are becalmed in clearest days,
　And in rough weather tossed ;
They wither under cold delays,
　Or are in tempests lost.

One while they seem to touch the port,
　Then straight into the main
Some angry wind in cruel sport
　Their vessel drives again.

At first disdain and pride they fear,
　Which, if they chance to 'scape,
Rivals and falsehood soon appear
　In a more dreadful shape.

By such degrees to joy they come,
  And are so long withstood,
So slowly they receive the sum,
  It hardly does them good.

'Tis cruel to prolong a pain,
  And to defer a bliss,
Believe me, gentle Celimene,
  No less inhuman is.

An hundred thousand oaths your fears
  Perhaps would not remove,
And if I gazed a thousand years,
  I could no deeper love.

'Tis fitter much for you to guess
  Than for me to explain,
But grant, Oh ! grant that happiness,
  Which only does remain.

(167)

JOHN DRYDEN.

No, no, poor suffering heart, no change endeavour,
Choose to sustain the smart, rather than leave her ;
My ravished eyes behold such charms about her,
I can die with her, but not live without her ;
One tender sigh of hers to see me languish,
Will more than pay the price of my past anguish :
Beware, O cruel fair, how you smile on me,
'Twas a kind look of yours that has undone me.

Love has in store for me one happy minute,
And she will end my pain who did begin it ;
Then no day void of bliss, or pleasure, leaving,
Ages shall slide away without perceiving :
Cupid shall guard the door, the more to please us,
And keep out Time and Death, when they would
    seize us :
Time and Death shall depart, and say, in flying,
Love has found out a way to live by dying.

(168)

EARL OF ROCHESTER.

ABSENT from thee I languish still,
  Then ask me not, when I return?
The straying fool 'twill plainly kill
  To wish all day, all night to mourn.

Dear, from thine arms then let me fly,
  That my fantastic mind may prove
The torments it deserves to try,
  That tears my fixed heart from my love.

When, wearied with a world of woe,
  To thy safe bosom I retire,
Where love, and peace, and honour flow,
  May I, contented, there expire.

Lest once more wandering from that heaven,
  I fall on some base heart unblessed,
Faithless to thee, false, unforgiven,
  And lose my everlasting rest.

(169)

JOHN DRYDEN.

THYRSIS.

FAIR Iris and her swain
  Were in a shády bower ;
Where Thyrsis long in vain
  Had sought the shepherd's hour :
At length his hand advancing upon her snowy breast;
  He said, O kiss me longer,
  And longer yet, and longer,
    If you will make me blest.

IRIS.

An easy yielding maid,
  By trusting, is undone ;
Our sex is oft betrayed,
  By granting love too soon.
If you desire to gain me, your sufferings to redress,
  Prepare to love me longer,
  And longer yet, and longer,
    Before you shall possess.

THYRSIS.

The little care you show
  Of all my sorrows past,
Makes death appear too slow,
  And life too long to last.
Fair Iris, kiss me kindly, in pity of my fate;
  And kindly still, and kindly,
    Before it be too late.

IRIS.

You fondly court your bliss,
  And no advances make;
'Tis not for maids to kiss,
  But 'tis for men to take.
So you may kiss me kindly, and I will not rebel;
  And kindly still, and kindly,
    But kiss me not and tell.

CHORUS.

A Rondeau.

Thus at the height we love and live,
  And fear not to be poor;
We give, and give, and give, and give,
  . Till we can give no more.
But what to-day will take away,
  To-morrow will restore.
Thus at the height we love and live,
  And fear not to be poor.

(170)

SIR EDWARD SHERBURNE.

A kiss I begg'd : but smiling, she
      Denied it me :
When straight, her cheeks with tears o'erflown
      (Now kinder grown),
What smiling she'd not let me have
      She weeping gave.
Then you whom scornful beauties awe
      Hope yet relief
From Love, who tears from smiles can draw,
      Pleasure from grief.

(171)

Sir Charles Sedley

Phillis is my only joy,
　Faithless as the winds or seas,
Sometimes cunning, sometimes coy,
　Yet she never fails to please;
　　　　If with a frown
　　　　I am cast down,
　　　　Phillis smiling
　　　　And beguiling
Makes me happier than before.

Though alas! too late I find
　Nothing can her fancy fix,
Yet the moment she is kind
　I forgive her all her tricks;
　　　　Which though I see,
　　　　I can't get free,—
　　　　She deceiving,
　　　　I believing,
What need lovers wish for more!

(172)

JOHN DRYDEN.

FAREWELL, fair Armida, my joy and my grief!
In vain I have loved you, and hope no relief,
Undone by your virtue, too strict and severe,
Your eyes gave me love, and you gave me despair.
Now called by my honour, I seek with content
The fate which in pity you would not prevent.
To languish in love were to find by delay
A death that 's more welcome the speediest way.

On seas and in battles, in bullets and fire,
The danger is less than in hopeless desire.
My death's wound you give me, though far off I bear
My fall from your sight, not to cost you a tear;
But if the kind flood on a wave should convey,
And under your window my body should lay,
The wound on my breast when you happen to see,
You 'll say with a sigh—It was given by me!

(173)

EARL OF ROCHESTER

VULCAN, contrive me such a cup
  As Nestor us'd of old;
Show all thy skill to trim it up,
  Damask it round with gold.

Make it so large, that, fill'd with sack
  Up to the swelling brim,
Vast toasts on the delicious lake,
  Like ships at sea, may swim.

Engrave not battle on his cheek,
  With war I 've nought to do,
I'm none of those that took Maestrick,
  Nor Yarmouth leaguer knew.

Let it no name of planets tell,
  Fix'd stars, or constellations;
For I am no Sir Sidrophel,
  Nor none of his relations.

But carve thereon a spreading vine,
  Then add two lovely boys ;
Their limbs in amorous folds entwine,
  The type of future joys.

Cupid and Bacchus my saints are,
  May Drink and Love still reign !
With wine I wash away my care,
  And then to love again.

(174)

JOHN DRYDEN.

ASK not the cause, why sullen Spring
    So long delays her flowers to bear;
Why warbling birds forget to sing,
    And winter storms invert the year;
Chloris is gone, and Fate provides
To make it spring, where she resides.

Chloris is gone, the cruel fair;
    She cast not back a pitying eye;
But left her lover in despair,
    To sigh, to languish, and to die.
Ah, how can those fair eyes endure,
To give the wounds they will not cure?

Great god of love, why hast thou made
    A face that can all hearts command,

That all religions can invade,
    And change the laws of every land?
Where thou hadst placed such power before,
Thou shouldst have made her mercy more.

When Chloris to the temple comes,
    Adoring crowds before her fall;
She can restore the dead from tombs,
    And every life but mine recall.
I only am by love designed
To be the victim for mankind.

(175)

EDMUND WALLER.

FAIR! that you may truly know,
What you unto Thyrsis owe;
I will tell you how I do
Sacharissa love, and you.
　　Joy salutes me when I set
My blest eyes on Amoret:
But with wonder I am strook,
While I on the other look.
　　If sweet Amoret complains,
I have sense of all her pains:
But for Sacharissa I,
Do not only grieve, but die.
　　All that of myself is mine
Lovely Amoret! is thine.
Sacharissa's captive fain
Would untie his iron chain;
And, those scorching beams to shun,
To thy gentle shadow run.

If the soul had free election
To dispose of her affection ;
I would not thus long have borne
Haughty Sacharissa's scorn :
But 'tis sure some power above
Which controls our wills in love !

If not a love, a strong desire
To create and spread that fire
In my breast, solicits me,
Beauteous Amoret ! for thee.

'Tis amazement, more than love,
Which her radiant eyes do move :
If less splendour wait on thine,
Yet they so benignly shine,
I would turn my dazzled sight
To behold their milder light.
But as hard 'tis to destroy
That high flame, as to enjoy :
Which how eas'ly I may do,
Heaven (as eas'ly seal'd) does know !

Amoret ! as sweet and good
As the most delicious food,
Which, but tasted, does impart
Life and gladness to the heart.

Sacharissa 's beauty's wine,
Which to madness doth incline :
Such a liquor, as no brain
That is mortal can sustain.

Scarce can I to Heaven excuse
The devotion, which I use
Unto that adorèd dame :
For 'tis not unlike the same,
Which I thither ought to send,
So that if it could take end,
'Twould to Heaven itself be due,
To succeed her, and not you :
Who already have of me
All that 's not idolatry :
Which, though not so fierce a flame,
Is longer like to be the same.
    Then smile on me, and I will prove
Wonder is shorter-liv'd than love.

(176)

JOHN DRYDEN.

CHLOE found Amyntas lying,
  All in tears, upon the plain,
Sighing to himself, and crying,
  'Wretched I, to love in vain!
Kiss me, dear, before my dying;
  Kiss me once, and ease my pain.'

Sighing to himself, and crying,
  'Wretched I, to love in vain!
Ever scorning, and denying
  To reward your faithful swain:
Kiss me, dear, before my dying;
  Kiss me once, and ease my pain!

'Ever scorning, and denying
  To reward your faithful swain.'

Chloe, laughing at his crying,
　Told him, that he loved in vain.
'Kiss me, dear, before my dying;
　Kiss me once, and ease my pain!'

Chloe, laughing at his crying,
　Told him that he loved in vain;
But repenting, and complying,
　When he kissed, she kissed again:
Kissed him up before his dying;
　Kissed him up, and eased his pain.

(177)

CHARLES COTTON.

FORBEAR, fair Phillis, oh forbear
Those deadly killing frowns, and spare
A heart so loving, and so true,
By none to be subdu'd, but you,
Who my poor life's sole princess are.
You only can create my care ;
But offend you, I all things dare ;
Then, lest your cruelty you rue,
              Forbear ;
And lest you kill that heart, beware,
To which there is some pity due,
If but because I humbly sue.
Your anger, therefore, sweetest fair,
Though mercy in your sex is rare,
              Forbear.

(178)

JOHN DRYDEN.

FAIR, sweet and young, receive a prize
Reserved for your victorious eyes :
From crowds, whom at your feet you see,
O pity, and distinguish me !
As I from thousand beauties more
Distinguish you, and only you adore.

Your face for conquest was designed,
Your every motion charms my mind ;
Angels, when you your silence break,
Forget their hymns to hear you speak ;
But when at once they hear and view,
Are loth to mount, and long to stay with you.

No graces can your form improve,
But all are lost, unless you love ;
While that sweet passion you disdain,
Your veil and beauty are in vain :
In pity then prevent my fate,
For, after dying, all reprieve 's too late.

(179)

EARL OF ROCHESTER.

My dear mistress has a heart
   Soft as those kind looks she gave me ;
When, with love's resistless art,
   And her eyes, she did enslave me ;
But her constancy 's so weak,
   She 's so wild and apt to wander,
That my jealous heart would break
   Should we live one day asunder.

Melting joys about her move,
   Killing pleasures, wounding blisses,
She can dress her eyes in love,
   And her lips can arm with kisses ;
Angels listen when she speaks,
   She 's my delight, all mankind's wonder,
But my jealous heart would break
   Should we live one day asunder.

(180)

JOHN DRYDEN.

YOU twice ten hundred deities,
To whom we daily sacrifice ;
You Powers that dwell with fate below,
And see what men are doomed to do,
Where elements in discord dwell ;
Then God of Sleep arise and tell
Great Zempoalla what strange fate
Must on her dismal vision wait.
By the croaking of the toad,
In their caves that make abode ;
Earthy, dun, that pants for breath,
With her swelled sides full of death ;
By the crested adder's pride,
That along the clifts do glide ;
By thy visage fierce and black ;
By the death's head on thy back ;
By the twisted serpents placed
For a girdle round thy waist ;
By the hearts of gold that deck
Thy breast, thy shoulders, and thy neck :
From thy sleepy mansion rise,
And open thy unwilling eyes,
While bubbling springs their music keep,
That use to lull thee in thy sleep.

(181)

CHARLES COTTON.

FAIR Isabel, if aught but thee
   I could, or would, or like, or love ;
   If other beauties but approve
To sweeten my captivity :
   I might those passions be above—
      Those pow'rful passions, that combine
      To make and keep me only thine.

Or, if for tempting treasure, I
   Of the world's god, prevailing gold,
   Could see thy love and my truth sold,
A greater, nobler treasury :
   My flame to thee might then grow cold,
      And I, like one whose love is sense,
      Exchange thee for convenience.

But when I vow to thee, I do
   Love thee above or health or peace,

Gold, joy, and all such toys as these,
'Bove happiness and honour too :
  Then thou must know, this love can cease
    Nor change, for all the glorious show
    Wealth and discretion bribes us to.

What such a love deserves, thou, sweet,
  As knowing best, may'st best reward :
  I, for thy bounty well prepar'd,
With open arms my blessing meet.
    Then do not, dear, our joys retard ;
      But unto him propitious be,
      That knows no love, nor life, but thee.

(182)

JOHN DRYDEN.

AH, fading joy! how quickly art thou past!
    Yet we thy ruin haste.
As if the cares of human life were few,
    We seek out new:
And follow fate which would too fast pursue.

See how on every bough the birds express
In their sweet notes their happiness.
They all enjoy and nothing spare,
But on their mother nature lay their care:
Why then should man, the lord of all below,
Such troubles choose to know,
As none of all his subjects undergo?

Hark, hark, the waters fall, fall, fall;
And with a murmuring sound
Dash, dash, upon the ground,
　To gentle slumbers call.

NOTES

P. 1.

This admirable poem was first printed in Davison's *Poetical Rhapsody* (1600). It is not certainly known to be Donne's, but all the best judges assign it to him, not merely on the internal evidence of the last stanza, but on early MS. authority, In some of the editions of the *Poetical Rhapsody* the piece is headed by an argument-couplet

> That time and absence proves
> Rather helps than hurts to loves.

P. 9.

It has been suspected that this piece, also, is Donne's, and it is worthy of him, though less in his style than in that of Ben. There are other versions and other readings, but this is the best. One text, printed from MS. by Dr. Grosart, has two additional verses, but they are only a feeble amplification of these.

P. 10.

The 'subtle wreath' is again referred to in *The Relique*. The line containing the reference

> A bracelet of bright hair about the bone

X

is one of the most famous and beautiful of all Donne's ; but the poem as a whole is inferior to this.

P. 12.

From the *Shoemaker's Holiday*.   This is one of my borrowings from the sixteenth century ; but Dekker specially belongs to the seventeenth.

P. 14.

Not very probably Raleigh's ; but attributed to him.
Gate.—A common form for ' gait.'

P. 22.

This is one of the things which, if Campion had been as bad a man as he seems to have been a good one, would rescue him from the grasp of the Black Cherubim and carry him to Paradise, with Mr. Arber, his partial, and Mr. Bullen, his complete, editors clinging to his skirts.

P. 23.

This and No. 15 are from *Deuteromelia* (1609).

P. 24.

Salathiel Pavy, the subject of this, was a ' Child of the Chapel Royal,' and therefore also an actor.

P. 25.

Not ' written the night before his execution,' but probably at least a dozen years earlier.

P. 27.

The last two lines are possibly spurious.

P. 32.

Said to have been 'found written in his Bible in the gate-house at Westminster,' and perhaps really his 'Last Wishes.'

P. 42.

As in many cases in this volume it is by no means certain whether Robert Jones wrote or borrowed the lyrics which he published and set to music. But some of them are among the best of their kind.

P. 48.

From Davison's *Poetical Rhapsody.* This could not easily be bettered ; but it does not seem to be known who wrote it.

P. 54.

I prefer the old-fashioned double attribution of 'Beaumont and Fletcher' as a general heading, wherever it is possible.

P. 55.

The lengthened fourth lines of stanzas 3 and 5 are notable in so careful a writer as Ben.

P. 66.

Wigge, or whig.—Soured whey or buttermilk.

P. 68.

Stanza 1, l. 6, of this exquisite song is a very little obscure. Some read 'and' for 'in' in l. 5, but I think 'in' better. They blush, but nothing awaits them save honour.

P. 70.

l. 16, 'By' seems to mean 'into the bargain.'

P. 75.

This magnificent descant was discovered by Mr. Bullen in a MS. music-book at Christ Church, Oxford, and first printed in his *More Lyrics from Elizabethan Song-Books.* I should not have reprinted it here without the leave which he most kindly gave me. With him most readers will cry *Aut Silurista aut diabolus*: and yet the breath of the Lord of lyric was so widely diffused then that we cannot be certain of Vaughan's authorship.

P. 92.

There may be some readers who will like this poem as well as all but the very finest things in the book. Its sentiment has been more prosaically summarised in the words, 'Oh! you are getting on too fast!'

P. 96.

Mazer—a wooden bowl.

P. 103.

Found by Mr. Bullen in a book of Airs by Captain Tobias Hume (1605), and justly extolled by him.

P. 108.

Maukin.—In this sense a cloth for cleaning a baker's oven ; or a cloth for cleaning generally.

P. 118.

From *Wit's Recreations.*

P. 119.

Epact.—Let him who knows not this word consult his Prayer-Book.

P. 121.

This song occurs both in Jones's *Musical Dream,* 1609, and in Campion's *Second Book of Airs,* 1613. The latter version was reprinted by Mr. Arber in the third volume of his *English Garner* (1880), and by Mr. Bullen in his *Works of Campion* (1889). In the *Lyrics from Elizabethan Song-Books* (1887) Mr. Bullen printed Jones's version, which is here followed. The variants in the other are very slight : 'may' for 'must' in l. 2, 'that' for 'which' in l. 4, and so on throughout. The second stanza in Campion runs thus :

> Your wished sight if I desire
> Suspicious you pretend,
> Causeless you yourself retire
> While I in vain attend.
> This a lover whets, you say,
> Still made more eager by delay.

P. 129.

The antithesis between 'Wit' and 'Will' runs through all the Elizabethan and earlier Jacobean writers ; and perhaps only a very extensive reading of them, or an elaborate excursus on the subject, could put the reader in a position to seize the various ramifications and up-croppings of it.   There is no space here for the excursus : I can heartily exhort to the reading.

P. 130.

I should like to read in the penultimate line—

> Till Time, too late, will make them cry.

P. 134.

Plats.—Doctors differ as to the meaning of this word here. I prefer the ordinary sense of 'plot,' as in garden-plot.

Melancholy streams.—The apparent meaning is that the noise of the flowing waters, melancholy in itself, gives pleasure to men—which is true enough.

P. 135.

Best of men.—Cotton, to whom the poem was addressed.
Old Greek.—Not the language but the liquor.
What.—Lovelace was not the most careful of writers.   But he might have defended this use of 'what' for 'which' or 'that' as short for 'whatsoever.'

P. 139.

Yet my lips.—Mr. Bullen, I think rightly, prefers this couplet to the mere repetition of 'Guess I can,' which also occurs.

P. 148.

The Great Marquess's verses are amateurish beyond all doubt, and the present piece is defaced by the political flings at 'synods' and 'committees.'   But the root of the matter is in it.

P. 151.

Coll = 'put your hands round my neck.'
Clip = 'embrace me round the body.'
Our cold affection. —In original 'out.'   The text is Mr. Bullen's reading, but I am not quite sure of it.

P. 160.

May.—Of course = 'girl.'   This charming word is less com·mon at the time than one might expect.

P. 172.

This early form of the 'Three Jolly Post-Boys' deserves reverence from the lovers of that noble ditty.   But I am told that even undergraduates do not know the 'Jolly Post-Boys' now.

> There's none that cups and cans it :
> The word is but, *Sic Transit.*

P. 173.

And here is another great original, that of Wordsworth's Ode of Odes.

P. 174.

Of course there is a temptation to read in the last line *into*. But Vaughan probably meant the break of metre.

P. 189.

Pomander—pomme d'ambre—a scent-box carried in the hand or pocket.

P. 199.

I should suspect :

> Soonest he wins, *he* fastest flies.

P. 205.

Yet shall no finger lose.—It is rather amusing to think of the ingenuity which commentators might spend on this apparently odd phrase if the facts were not known.   As it is, the explanation is grovellingly simple : Randolph himself had lost a finger in a fray.

P. 207.

Warrants.—Alluding to the practice of granting favoured persons warrants for a buck, or more than one, from royal forests.   Below Mr. Hazlitt reads ' all are,' but the older reading ' are all ' is better metre, and quite good enough sense.

P. 211.

Stench.—Of course but another form of ' stanch.'   This beautiful song is sung by Pangloretta, the temptress, in *Christ's Triumph on Earth.*

P. 217.

I have made too many anthologies myself to quarrel much with omissions or exclusions in those of others.   But I have never ceased to wonder at the exclusion of this master-piece, the very type of its kind, from Mr. Palgrave's *Golden Treasury.*

P. 222.

Matchavil.—Of course = 'Machiavel'; and in common quotation of the line, a favourite one, it is usually spelt so. But Cowley must have intended the oddity, perhaps for a play on 'match.'

P. 223.

I do not care much for this famous poem ; but I suppose it would be missed, and its author is very hard to sample otherwise.

P. 228.

The second quatrain of the second stanza here is grammatically licentious, but the meaning is clear enough. *' To enjoy '* or *' to receive which '* is perhaps the simplest filling up.

P. 232.

Register = ' registrar.' *Con* = ' acknowledge.' This pretty piece perhaps comes to an end, as far as general interest is concerned, with the preceding stanza. William Chourne of Staffordshire, and Cureton, and Broker, are but as ' Henry Pimpernel and old John Naps of Greece ' to us. But I have made it a principle not to mutilate.

P. 234.

There are divers various readings in this poem of which I do not think it necessary to take note here. One, however, ' far ' for ' fair ' before ' Amphion ' on the next page, seems probable.

P. 240.

Sinople = ' vert ' in foreign heraldry.   Here again, as generally
in Drummond, there are various readings, and ll. 6 and 7
seem corrupt.   Perhaps l. 6 should read with brackets and a
note of exclamation, as a parenthetical ejaculation.

P. 247.

Sydneian showers. —The attraction of Sir Philip Sidney's
conversation is repeatedly referred to in the *Tombeau*, or collection of funeral poems on Astrophel, usually printed in Spenser's
Works.

P. 249.

Story = ' history.'

P. 250.

This most musical song is not continuous in its original place,
The Inner Temple Masque, the stanzas being interrupted by a
longish dialogue between the Siren and Triton.

P. 253.

Many bad things have been said, some truly, some falsely, of
Macaulay : but I know hardly anything for which I find it so
difficult to forgive him as his remarks on Sedley's verse.

P. 256.

I think this is the first time (for collections of Dramatic
Lyrics, or Songs from Dramatists hardly count) that Dryden's
Lyrics have had a fair show with those of his peers ; and I
am not afraid of the result, even though one or two of his very
best are not producible here.

P. 263.

A quaint and pleasing poem, which shows 'hearty, cheerful Mr. Cotton' at almost the best of his curious blend of thoroughly poetical conception with imperfect poetical execution.

P. 265.

One is tempted to give almost everything presentable of Rochester's often magnificent metre and phrase. Yet one of the examples which begins best, the famous

> An age, in her embraces past,
> Would seem a winter's day,

ends but lamely; and in such a collection the representation of poets of the second order must be limited, especially where there is a strong disinclination to mutilate.

P. 268.

I am not sure that the refrain does not read best, 'a Ha, ha, ha, ha !'

P. 280.

In second stanza v. 1. 'joy' for 'bliss,' and last line, 'Offends the wingèd boy.'

P. 281.

One of Dryden's latest, and one of his best songs.

P. 285.

The last distich of this pretty poem of Sherburne (Carew's moon) is obviously misprinted in Chalmers's *Poets*.

P. 303.

An early song of Dryden's (from the *Indian Emperor*) but a matchless finale, if only for the one line—

And follow fate which would too fast pursue.

INDEX OF AUTHORS